Zaria Fierce and the Enchanted Drakeland Sword

By Keira Gillett

Reading Order:

Zaria Fierce and the Secret of Gloomwood Forest

Zaria Fierce and the Enchanted Drakeland Sword

Praise for Zaria Fierce and the Secret of Gloomwood Forest

"Are you in the mood for an old fashioned magical jaunt? Zaria Fierce and the Secret of Gloomwood Forest by Keira Gillett is a classic "perilous adventure" book for middle grade readers." *Jennifer Bardsley, The YA Gal*

"A captivating blending of fantasy storytelling with today's technology. At the base of this tale is deep, abiding friendship that stands the tests of time, adventure and even danger." *Kathy Haw, Goodreads Review*

"A great book with a lovely story and amazing characters. It's a fantasy and adventure book that will be the delight of Narnia fans and those looking for a bit of Norwegian folklore thrown into it." *Ner, A Cup of Coffee and a Book*

"If you're looking for an action-packed adventure dipped in fantasy, look no further. This book kept me on my toes with its many cliffhangers and plot twists; it was quite hard to put down at times." *Meredith, All 'Bout Them Books and Stuff*

"I love when a story jumps right in and hooks me like this one did. I highly recommend you look into it if you are in the mood for a fun adventure. I also recommend that you get it for any book loving middle schooler you know." *Emily, Midwestern Book Nerd*

Dedication:

I dedicate this book to my family and friends (old and new) who willingly jumped onto the Zaria Fierce bandwagon with boundless enthusiasm. I can't begin to express how much it has meant to me. Thank you for all the love you've put into the series.

To Readers:

Zaria Fierce continues to surprise me. Happy coincidences have added so much more depth to the world. Heave ho and climb on board! We're off to explore magical Norway some more.

Table of Contents

Prologue: The Keenness
to Tackle Dragons

Zaria woke again with the feeling of self-loathing. She stared at the ceiling recalling last night's theatrical performance of Shakespeare's *A Midsummer Night's Dream,* which she attended in Oslo with her parents. The antics of Puck, a mischievous fairy, had failed to lighten her mood. The urge to punch something often overcame her and she struggled to keep a rein on her overwrought emotions. She knew why she was angry, but she didn't know how to stop being angry.

She rolled over, stuffing her pillow under her head. She felt so hopeless and was ashamed to admit it, convinced she didn't have a right to complain. Hector had told her to stay put, but there was nothing worse, she thought, than being forced into inaction. It didn't help that news from him was infrequent and slim on details. She wanted to help, but she didn't know where to start.

She was new to the magical world of Norway, even if she'd been born a part of it. She learned she was a princess, and her birth mother, Queen Helena, was a sorceress who ruled the Under Realm and guarded the world from dragons, whose powers could sway nations.

Her earlier zeal to save her Chinese friend, Christoffer, had led her to being tricked into handing over Hart, the son of Hector – the Stag Lord of the ellefolken, – to a nasty river-troll, named Olaf. Now Hart was in the hands of Koll, the worst of the dragons, and his allies, while she anxiously waited for word from Hector as to how she and her friends could free him. Their only hope to find him was a special arrow-heart shaped necklace once worn by Hart, which Hector now wore.

Saving Hart wasn't her only problem though. Olaf was determined to set Koll free from his prison. There were four pieces of the puzzle that the river-troll needed to solve. He had one with Hart. He also needed the Drakeland Sword and a pair of charmed shoes (and the secret to removing them). Zaria, too, was one of the things Olaf needed, but she didn't really understand what that meant. She knew she would never willingly help Olaf, but that hadn't seemed to matter eight months ago.

She wanted to beat Olaf at his own game, but the gung-ho attitude to run off half-cocked was no longer there. That was the problem with waiting, she mused. Waiting inevitably cooled impulsiveness, and she missed the fire the initial zeal had given her. If she could do something to help, Zaria knew the pain and guilt she felt for her actions last November would lessen.

So Zaria prepared, keeping a backpack filled with clean clothes, including her favorite pair of pajamas with little foxes, travel toiletries, prepackaged food, a flashlight, batteries, and maps, although these maps were not the vintage ones her adoptive father had given her for her birthday two years ago. The mountain-trolls still had them somewhere in Trolgar (and she wanted them back.) The maps she now carried were photocopies from atlases and various books of fairy tales. Zaria didn't know what would be handy, but she wanted to cover all her bases.

It was the second week of July, and it was more than time for the next adventure. But when exactly would it start? Christoffer was impatient, having missed the last one. Their other friends were also anxious. And Zaria? Well, Zaria was ready to take on dragons.

Chapter One: A Nightly Disturbance

Zaria closed the book she was reading with a sigh and tossed it on the nightstand beside her bed. She took a moment to stretch luxuriously before standing. She wondered where Christoffer was. He usually escaped his parents' overbearing attention once or twice a week and would skip off to one of his friend's places. She thought he'd come by tonight.

Deciding to get a glass of water, Zaria walked across her bedroom. As she reached the door a sharp crack sounded against her window causing her to jump and spin around. The cause of the disturbance became clear when a second stone bounced off the glass.

Racing across the room, Zaria reached the window and peered through the curtains. Below her stood Christoffer, sporting a grin and wearing a navy blue captain's hat over his spikey black hair. He waved as Zaria threw the window open, letting in a rush of cool night air.

Leaning out of her second floor window, Zaria called down, "Is the front door too inconvenient for you?"

"I've sprung from my parents," he said happily. "God knows I love them, but I am going stir crazy with all their attention. I am ready for some fun. Let me up."

Zaria stretched and released the fire escape ladder. It fell with a sharp *bang*. Christoffer quickly mounted and climbed, the sleeves of his navy blue jacket getting in the way. When he reached Zaria, she backed away from the window to let him into the room. He ducked through the opening and slung his arms around Zaria in a loose hug.

"Any news?" he asked.

Zaria shook her head. "Nothing new."

Christoffer sighed unhappily. He was as disappointed as she was by the lack of news. He wanted to be a part of the adventure to come – had in fact, made

Zaria promise to bring him with her when the time came.

It would be a challenge to get him away from his parents, but they would manage it. It helped that they had a special device in their possession which would aid their absconding when the time came.

"Hector's bound to send you something soon though, right?" Christoffer asked, tilting the hat further back on his head. He looked rather jaunty.

"He was a regular correspondent up until he went to Jötunheim."

"The giants, right?"

Zaria nodded and sat down on the bed. "I think it's because it's so far away. I don't even know how he gets the mail to me. It just shows up in our mailbox. Mom read over my shoulder last time I got a letter. It was about Hector and his team hunting for trolls."

"What did she say to that?"

"Of course she wanted to know what it meant. I told her that it was a pen-pal story project for school. She thought it was highly creative and asked to read the final copy."

"I wonder how tall they are," Christoffer mused, sitting on the floor and leaning against her bookcase.

"The giants?" Zaria asked.

"Yeah," he said.

She thought for a moment and guessed, "They have to be tall enough that when they make furniture in miniature, it's perfectly sized for us."

Christoffer whistled. "So compare us to dollhouse furniture, and it's about the same isn't it?"

"What do you know about dollhouse furniture?" Zaria teased.

Christoffer shrugged. "My twin sisters have gobs of that stuff lying around."

Zaria reached over to her nightstand and picked up her phone. "I'm going to Google the ratio of dollhouse furniture to normal furniture."

"Cool," Christoffer said just as his phone started to vibrate in his pocket. He sighed gustily when a photo of his mother flashed across the screen. "Hi Mum," he said, then paused and winced, knocking his hat to the floor. "I'm at Zaria's…. No, her parents don't know I'm here…. fire escape…. No, you don't have to pick me up…. Please don't…. Okay, okay. I'm leaving now. See you soon…. Yeah, love you too. Bye, Mum." He rolled his eyes at Zaria as he hung up. "She's driving me crazy."

"She's just worried. Cut her some slack."

Christoffer grabbed his hat replacing it firmly on his head. "I've got to go. Did you figure out the ratio?"

"One place said it was a twelve-to-one ratio."

"So giants are what –" Christoffer looked up and tallied in his head. "Something like twenty-two meters… er… that's what, seventy-two feet tall? Wow. We'd be like squirrels to them."

Zaria squinted and shook her head. "No, probably not. Isn't seventy-two feet more like the size of a tree? Giants are tall, but not so tall we'd be like squirrels to them. Squirrels are squirrels to them."

Christoffer laughed and slid open the window. He ducked through in a blink of an eye and was gone. Zaria leaned out and watched him descend the metal ladder. When he reached the bottom he gave her a thumbs-up. She pulled the ladder up from the ground.

"Night, Zaria," he called, turning to leave.

"Good night, Christoffer. Text me when you get home!"

He waved to acknowledge her request without turning around. When he reached the head of the alleyway he paused. Turning back, he glanced up at Zaria framed in the window where she stood watching.

Cupping his hands to his mouth, Christoffer yelled. "We're going to the Tall Ships Race tomorrow. Want to come?"

Zaria smiled and nodded. "Yes!" she shouted back.

And with that he was gone.

She pulled away from the window and shut it before going to get the glass of water she'd wanted earlier. In the hallway she met Merry, her adoptive mother, wearing a fluffy blue bathrobe and gray bunny slippers. Even dressed for bed, Merry was a beautiful and warm Indian woman with big brown eyes, dark glossy hair, and clear caramel-colored skin.

"Mrs. Johansen called. She wanted to make sure that Christoffer had left."

Zaria nodded. "He was only here for a few moments."

"Next time let me know, okay?" Merry asked gently, pulling her hair over her shoulder. "I had to tell Emma I would call her back. It makes me look bad if I don't know who's over."

"Sorry," Zaria said. "I would've gotten around to it, but his mum called him before I could."

"It's all right. Just remember for next time. Is he going to text you when he's back home?"

"He said he would."

"Let me know when he does. Do you want me to make you some tea? I was heading for the kitchen."

"Okay," Zaria said, following her mom.

Merry rang up Emma Johansen to let her know that Christoffer was on his way home. Then, they had some girl talk about nothing in particular while Zaria kept checking her mobile. She knew Christoffer would be safe to travel at night, because Olaf wasn't about to kidnap him twice. What would be the point? Still she would feel better once Christoffer texted her.

Anger crept over her, darkening her mood. She felt so hopeless about everything and nothing. She tried not to let her bad mood be apparent to her mom, but Merry was keenly perceptive.

She gave Zaria a few shortbread cookies to eat with her tea, and the sweet gesture helped to dissipate the bad mood that had stolen over her. It disappeared entirely not long after that when Christoffer texted his safe arrival home. She kissed her mom goodnight, prepared for bed, and planned her outfit for the Tall Ships Race event the next day, determined to be happier.

***

Zaria was enjoying herself immensely at the street party for the Tall Ships Race. It was an unusually warm sunny day. The wind from the Atlantic current was balmy. She wished she hadn't brought the light sweater Merry had insisted she bring. It was currently wrapped around her waist, as she ate cotton candy and stole popcorn from Filip. He didn't mind and would steal cotton candy as revenge.

As she wandered the streets with her friends, Zaria laughed in delight at some of the makeshift costumes people had worn. Filip, green-eyed, brash, and blond, liked what a twenty-something guy was wearing. It was a 3-D painted cardboard getup of a pirate ship over his clothes, complete with a black and white skull-and-bones flag, and held up by red suspenders.

The guy pretended to pilot it about, but it was an excuse to run wild as he bumped haphazardly into people like a pinball ricocheting around a course. It was fun to see how people reacted to him. Some were annoyed, but most wanted to take his picture and he proudly posed for them. It was the only time he stood still.

Geirr, tall, black, and preppy with vivid blue eyes, preferred a different costume. One man had constructed onto his skateboard a wooden toy ship with a center mast, which he held onto for balance as he scooted around the street. It even had working sails. He had what looked like a mop on his head, and a captain's hat worn backwards. Zaria liked the costume too and insisted that they waylay him and snag a photo for posterity.

Street music played energetically all over the wharf from different bands. Some were folksy, some party electronic, some big band, and some rock. Geirr and Christoffer argued about which band they should go visit next. Geirr wanted to go to the folksy group near one of the big ships. Christoffer wanted to hang out by the party electronic band at the center of the street and dance.

Aleks, their redheaded changeling friend, explained as they walked that the Tall Ships Race brought people from all over the globe. He was very much into tall ships. He and his grandpa (who was not married to Grams, his changeling grandmother) would rent out sailing ships every summer when his grandpa visited from Oslo.

The race, and in particular the crew battle, according to Aleks, was a highlight not to be missed. Zaria was inclined to agree with him as she watched crews move around the ships preparing them for the launch of the cruise-in-company part of the route. There were roughly seventy ships and twenty-five hundred crew entered in the regatta this year.

Zaria couldn't wait to watch the sails unfurl. It would be like watching a different era unfold before her eyes – a time of discovery, exploration, and pirates. Speaking of which, Aleks was so enthusiastic about the race he was dressed like a pirate with an eye-patch and red-striped shirt. His youthful freckled face was tanned from the sun and his smile bright.

When they came across a group of street performers teaching children how to walk on stilts it was a unanimous decision by the group to go over and try it out for themselves. They had a great time and made fun of each other's efforts.

Only Christoffer and Aleks got the hang of it and were soon walking around like pros. Geirr and Filip were decent, but would lose balance periodically and topple over. Zaria on the other hand was hopeless. She was proud of her efforts though, because she'd eventually been able to go about six steps before falling.

Zaria thanked and tipped the street performer who had assisted them, prompting the others to copy her. As they walked away, Filip slung his arms around Zaria's and Geirr's necks. Playfully, he tried to jump, swinging his feet into the air.

"Cut it out, mate," Geirr grumbled good-naturedly, digging his elbow into Filip's side.

"Ow," Filip complained. "Was that necessary?"

Geirr and Zaria locked eyes, bright blue meeting violet, and together said, "Yes!"

Filip's pout broke all three down into giggles.

"Guys," Aleks called to them from up ahead. "It's almost time! Come on!"

They raced over to where a group of Class A ships was moored. There were many classes, but the children were most excited to see the big ships that would sport many sails. They fought through the crowds that had gathered to spectate and clustered together in front of the biggest ship docked, the *Vikrant*. The ship was grand and majestic with its wooden deck creaking ever so slightly as it rocked on the waves.

Crew members in bright multicolored rain parkas and jackets worked diligently to untie ropes, climb the masts, and secure the sails. Over a bullhorn it was announced that the *Vikrant* would launch a series of firecrackers to celebrate their standing in the race.

"Two more legs to go," Aleks said, excitedly. He hoped the *Vikrant* would win, and it was possible it could, provided it beat out some of its competitors.

To Zaria it was like watching a pirate movie, without the pirates. Pity. It would have been fun if the crew dressed that way, like Aleks' had. It seemed like an opportunity missed.

Moments later the firecrackers started. The loud series of bangs and pops drew gasps from the crowd. The children pressed eagerly forward to see the show. Smoke billowed in the air. It hit Zaria's nose with an acridity that made her sneeze.

"Bless you, Princess," said a familiar voice behind her.

Zaria and her friends spun around. Christoffer gaped at the tall, blond, bearded man wearing a surprisingly normal ensemble with a brown leather jacket, faded blue jeans, a stone heart necklace on a leather cord, and mirrored sunglasses. Zaria gave the man a hug.

"Hector! Why are you here?" she asked when she pulled back.

Hector scratched his beard and gestured vaguely around. "I'm here to steal a ship."

Chapter Two: An
Expeditious Plan

"You're what?" Aleks demanded, aghast.

Hector gave Zaria a wink. The Stag Lord was pranking her friends and they hadn't caught on yet. She stifled a giggle.

"Cool," Christoffer said, enthused. "What can we do to help?"

Hector looked at Christoffer for a moment. "You're the friend they rescued, aren't you?"

Christoffer nodded. "Yeah. Sorry to hear about your son though. That was a rotten deal."

"Indeed," Hector agreed. He drew them aside, away from the crowd. "Children, you'll need to meet me at that spot over there in two hours."

Filip shaded his eyes and looked in the direction Hector was pointing. "At the mouth of the Glomma?"

"Yes, where the trees stand at the edge of the land," Hector replied. "I am meeting our navigator. He will take us through the Skagerrak, around the coast of Norway, and up to Seiland, the high court of Jötunheim."

"Why can't we ride on wyverns? Wouldn't they be faster?" Filip asked.

"They would be," Hector agreed. "We can't take them, however, because the elves and trolls need them for patrols. I even volunteered Norwick for Edevart's personal use."

"Wait! You're working with trolls now?" Geirr exclaimed. "But they're the bad guys!"

"King Kafirr might be a frequent challenger of the status quo, but he's less enemy and more of an annoying bully," Hector explained. "Like a child, he wants to rule over as many as he can and take any action with impunity. When we don't let him, he lashes out, especially if it's to his advantage."

"So why are you working with him again?" Geirr asked.

"When his forward guard broke treaty with Olaf, Kafirr was first to reach out to the others. He, Silje, and Hakon have reached an agreement that should be mutually beneficial to all."

"Silje?" Aleks asked. "Who's that?"

Zaria nudged Aleks' side. "She's the queen of the elves. Remember Frida mentioned her?"

"I remember the desserts," Filip said with a happy sigh. "Edevart is a lucky elf."

"Hakon's your father and a tree, right?" Christoffer butted-in. "How does that work?"

"Later," Hector said, waving Christoffer's question away. "Princess, you are needed. The dwarves refuse to honor their word regarding the Drakeland Sword unless you present yourself in their kingdom. They won't hand over the sword until they've verified you are Queen Helena's daughter."

"We better hurry then," Aleks said. He reached into his pocket. "I've got my stargazer on me. Should we activate it now?"

Hector shook his head. "No, it is best we don't. Magic like that has its limits. You used much of it on your last adventure. Wait until we leave. Be safe."

***

The friends rushed along the streets and over the river, taking the shortest path over the scrollwork bridge that had started their last adventure. Olaf did not jump out to greet them. Not that Zaria expected him to, not now that she had her hard-won freedom to cross his river. He'd gotten Hart and hadn't been seen or heard from since.

On the other side, Zaria and Filip split off from the others to turn left toward their homes. They stopped at Zaria's first to pick up her backpack; she was happy she'd had the forethought to pack a bag and keep it at the ready. It would save them time. She dashed into the apartment and toward her bedroom.

"Back so soon?" Merry asked, stepping out of the kitchen with a coffee mug in her hand. She wore a pale blue sari with silver stitching. "Did you have a good time?"

In a blink of an eye, Zaria was back in the hallway with her backpack. She kissed her mom on the cheek. "It's been great. Christoffer's parents are inviting everyone over for a sleepover after the street party breaks up. I'm just grabbing my stuff."

"Aren't you going to ask permission first?" Merry teased.

Zaria immediately put on her most contrite expression and asked sweetly, "Mom, you know I love you, right?"

"Yes," she said wryly. "Normally, this is where I would ask you what you want."

"But you already know what I want. May I go? Please? Please?" Zaria begged.

Merry gathered her into a hug. "Of course you may, sweetie. You packed in a hurry. Are you sure you have everything?"

Zaria nodded. "You bet. I had an idea that a sleepover might come up, so I packed ahead."

Merry laughed and kissed her daughter on the cheek. "Off you go then. Please text me throughout the evening so I know you're all right."

"Will do! Love you for real, Mom!"

"I love you too, honey."

Outside, Zaria caught up with Filip and they ran through the streets to his house. His front door was unlocked. His mother glanced up from her seat on the sofa. She set aside her book and stood up with a smile.

"Hello, Zaria," she greeted.

"Hi, Mrs. Storstrand," Zaria said, shaking her hand as Filip pounded up the stairs.

"What brings you here?" asked the softly rounded woman. She had the same blonde hair and green eyes as her son, but that's where the resemblance ended. "It was my understanding you were at the Tall Ships Race with Emma and Zhuang."

Zaria shrugged, trying to keep the heat of incrimination off her face. She didn't have this problem with her mom (but mostly because she knew her mom would understand the small deception).

"They invited us to a slumber party. Mr. and Mrs. Johansen are walking the others home to collect their things. Filip and I thought we could go by ourselves because we live in the opposite direction of everyone. I hope you don't mind."

Mrs. Storstrand sighed. "Well, to be honest, I was expecting Filip home this evening. His older brother is returning tonight from Uni."

Zaria ducked her head abashed. "Sorry, I didn't know."

"He did," Mrs. Storstrand said with a grimace. "I'll be right back, Zaria. Please wait here."

Zaria stood in the hallway feeling out of place and a little intrusive. She tucked her hands in her pockets and strove to hear anything up the stairs. The most she got were vague murmurs. A few moments later, Filip ran down the stairs with a mulish expression. Zaria feared the worst.

"Filip," Mrs. Storstrand called, coming down the stairs after him.

Filip grabbed Zaria's arm and tugged. "Let's go," he hissed.

Zaria dragged her feet, looking over her shoulder. "But, your mum –"

"– is being ridiculous," Filip muttered under his breath. Over his shoulder he said, "We're leaving. I'll text you later."

"Filip Gregory Storstrand, I'm not done talking with you. Come back here."

Extremely uncomfortable with the situation, Zaria edged closer to the door. She didn't want to see Filip fight with his mother. Filip sighed in frustration and returned to his mum. This time Zaria could hear everything and really wished she couldn't.

"It's not like Collin cares, Mum," Filip argued heatedly.

"You're staying. I let you go earlier to the street party for the race events, but you can't miss your brother. It'll hurt his feelings."

"He has his own friends he wants to see. I'm not going to miss hanging out with everyone just because you want to do a family thing tonight. I have a life."

"Filip, it is out of the question. Go put your backpack in your room. Stay there if you must, but when you come downstairs, you will be well-behaved and pleasant."

"But, Mum!"

"Enough. I don't want to hear any more. Say goodbye to Zaria."

Filip sulked and stomped back to Zaria. "Bye," he practically growled.

Zaria raised an eyebrow and crossed her arms. "Just because you're mad at your mother doesn't mean you should act snarly with me."

Filip scowled, but nodded. He closed his eyes and rolled his neck and shoulders until the tension dropped. When he opened his eyes again they were a friendly green.

He whispered, "Sorry. You're right of course. It's just so frustrating? Why now? This is so unfair. Mum normally lets me do what I want."

She sneaked a peek at Mrs. Storstrand who watched over them from the stairs. "Apparently not when it comes to family bonding time."

"Ugh," Filip groused. "Tell the others. I think we're going to need Aleks' device after all – not to spring Christoffer – but to spring me."

Zaria tipped her head in acknowledgement. Then she waved meekly at Mrs. Storstrand and said loudly, "I'm sorry you can't come tonight. There's always next time. I'll tell the others."

***

Zaria, Christoffer, Aleks, and Geirr crouched in the alley between Filip's house and the neighbor's. They had about thirty minutes before meeting Hector at the copse of trees. Christoffer grabbed a couple of rocks and tossed them at Filip's window with an ease born of much practice.

"Your aim is getting really good," Geirr commented. "Just be careful you don't break a window and give us away."

Christoffer threw him a cheeky smile. "Can't make any promises."

Filip slung his window open and tossed out his backpack. It landed in a thump in the hedgerow. Aleks pulled it out and slung it over his shoulder with his own bag.

"How're you getting down?"

"Hopefully with your stargazer."

"Then why toss down your bag?" Aleks asked, exasperated.

"Just in case," Filip said with a wink at Zaria.

She suppressed a smile. She looked to the others, "Does anybody have rope?"

Aleks and Geirr both nodded. Then Geirr unzipped his bag and pulled out a neat coil from on top. He tossed it to Filip, who snatched it up as it sailed by the window. He disappeared into his bedroom and reappeared moments later slinging the coil out the window. It unraveled to the ground.

"Good," Filip said briskly. "It's long enough. Now let's see if it holds."

Filip quickly scaled the side of the house and they gathered their belongings preparing to dash. Without warning, Mrs. Storstrand stuck her head out of a bottom window and shrieked at the sight of them.

"Just what do you think you're doing?" she demanded.

"Run!" Filip shouted, grabbing his friends' sleeves and rushing for the street.

Aleks cursed and threw Filip his backpack while slinging his own around to the front and unzipping a pocket. He looked frazzled as he dug inside the opening. Mrs. Storstrand was quick. She was already out of the house and chasing after them. She threatened life and limb and the most terrible of all – letting Filip's father know what he was about.

At last Aleks found the stargazer – a shiny purplish egg-shaped object perforated with stars – and almost dropped it in his haste. After a brief fumble, Aleks located the largest star, and hastily jabbed his finger into the hole. Just like that, Mrs. Storstrand froze mid-run. But so too did Christoffer, Filip, and Geirr.

Aleks looked at Zaria and to the others. "Damn," he hissed. "Wait! How are you not frozen too?"

Zaria shrugged. "Maybe because my birth mother is a sorceress? So I'm not human?"

"But I freeze when I'm not touching it and it's activated. I'm a changeling. I'm technically fey."

Zaria shrugged again. "How am I supposed to know? It's your stargazer. Maybe you've been right all along and you're more human than fey anymore."

"Maybe," Aleks conceded. He grabbed her arm and steered her to the others. He arranged them in a huddle. "Now hold onto these two," he said, pointing to Geirr and Filip.

Then he linked arms with Christoffer and Geirr, completing the circle, and with a little contortion pressed his pinky into the smallest star on the stargazer.

"Get back here right –"

Aleks hurriedly pressed the large star and cut Mrs. Storstrand off mid-rant. Filip was the first to relax. He grinned hugely at the others and high-fived Aleks.

"Awesome!"

"You're going to be in so much trouble," Zaria muttered.

"Totally worth it," Filip said, brushing his wavy blond hair off his forehead.

Christoffer shook his head in amazement. "Even the water from the neighbor's hose appears to have stopped. This is so cool. Remind me, why didn't we go outside before when we used the stargazer?"

"Because Grams made it sound like it wouldn't work," Aleks said, rolling his eyes, then added, "We should get going. There isn't much time to meet Hector."

"It's just too bad," Christoffer complained. "This whole city could have been ours!"

"Even though she told you it wouldn't work, do you think she knew it could?" Zaria asked.

"I doubt it," Aleks said as he stuffed the stargazer into his front pocket and started walking. The others followed, falling into step beside him.

"It wasn't much of a plan," Geirr commented, taking one last look over his shoulder at Mrs. Storstrand with her angry expression and raised fists. "But it did the job."

"Thanks for breaking me out, mate," Filip said, slapping Geirr and Aleks on the back. "Now it's adventure time!"

"Here, here," Christoffer chanted, excitement clear in his brown eyes and on his tan face. "Let's go!"

***

Hector was waiting for them with an impatient expression on his face. His arms were crossed and he kept checking the sky and water. Then he noticed their approach and waved them forward. They ran over and formed a loose semi-circle around him.

"Didn't I tell you not to use the stargazer yet?" Hector said sternly, giving Aleks a cross look.

Aleks looked at Filip and the others and back to Hector. "Sorry. Filip's mother wasn't going to let him go with us and we had to use it to get her to stop chasing us."

"You could have turned it off as soon as you had escaped around a corner and gone out of sight."

"We didn't think of that," Zaria said. "We can turn it off now."

Aleks started to pull the stargazer from his pocket.

"You'd just turn it on now," said Hector, staying his hand. "Don't worry about it. Your little device will either hold or it won't. Time will tell."

Aleks shrugged and stuffed the stargazer back in his pocket. "Works for me."

"Follow me, children. We're going out to the ship."

"Where is it?" Christoffer asked, looking to where the different tall ships were anchored.

Hector pointed to the left. "There."

He whistled. "Excellent!"

The ship was massive and quite impressive. It was fully rigged with the sails at half-mast. The body was painted cherry red with bold, bright-white script, which spelled *Ursula* along its side. It took Zaria's breath away.

"She's a beauty," Aleks said with a happy sigh. "At least ninety meters long."

"A hundred," Hector confirmed. "She's is a good strong vessel. We'll be fast on her. Come, here's our ride out to her."

A tender came alongside the shore where they stood. Aleks scrambled into the craft eagerly. He was more than ready to climb onboard *Ursula* and explore. Zaria navigated to her seat with help from Hector, and the others arranged themselves around the rest of the boat.

Zaria looked at their navigator, who was wearing a large oversized trench coat, and gasped. Her reaction drew Christoffer's gaze and he gasped too. Their navigator was a troll!

He looked a lot like Olaf with the blue-brown scales and slightly webbed hands. He must be a river-troll, too, as he lacked the tail and all-over shaggy fur of a mountain-troll. What was a river-troll doing on the sea?

Zaria continued to observe him as he greeted Hector with sheepish good cheer at Hector's profuse thanks. The boys noticed then that the ship hadn't been stolen after all. Christoffer complained to her under his breath. He'd been looking forward to a little piracy on the high seas.

She ignored him to study the navigator. To Zaria, the troll was shaped rather like a large dollop of cookie dough with two small fangs that dipped below his upper lip, which curled up in a slight smile. His large nose tapered into a sharp tip. But it was his eyes which relaxed Zaria, for they were warm and friendly. Beyond the superficial appearances of skin color and a few other features, this troll looked nothing like Olaf.

"Welcome, welcome," the river-troll said, shaking his shaggy hair out of his eyes, revealing short horns by his forehead. "I am Bjarke. We'll be embarking on my dear *Ursula* soon."

"She's yours?" Aleks asked, then tacked on eagerly, "Tell me about her. How many cabins? How many crew members? How tall is the main mast?"

Bjarke grinned in delight as he steered the tender toward his ship. "Ten cabins. Forty crew. Forty meters."

"Bjarke," Hector explained, "got out of the river business two hundred years ago. He runs *Ursula* up and down the Scandinavian territories, chartering cruises for humans, trolls, elves, fairies, dwarves, and sometimes a giant or two, if they're young or small. Although he isn't picky – he might help out the less desirables such as hags and banshees."

"My ship, my rules," Bjarke said, scratching his rounded belly.

"Why did you leave your river?" Zaria asked, curious. She tilted her head to look up at him, shielding her eyes from the sun.

Bjarke's face darkened. "Something unnatural happened. My river shrank; the waters turned gray; and the trees became twisted and dark along its banks. I could feel it begin to affect me so I left."

"Affect you?" Geirr questioned.

"Aye," Bjarke said solemnly. "It was like a disease of the mind. I was turning ugly and dark."

Hector listened, his face impassive, but Zaria noticed a tightening at the corners of his eyes. She wondered why Bjarke's story would disquiet him. She turned back to the troll with attentiveness. She wanted to know what Bjarke's story meant.

"Do you mind?" Christoffer piped up, standing in the troll's space.

Bjarke jumped and snarled, before calming himself. "Sorry, lad, ye scared me. Mind what?"

"Your skin, is it scales?" Christoffer asked bluntly. He was clearly fascinated.

Zaria blushed in embarrassment. "Christoffer you're being rude. You don't just ask somebody, if you can touch their skin because it's different from your own."

Bjarke looked at Christoffer with bemusement. "Haven't ye ever seen a troll before?"

Christoffer nodded sheepishly. "Yeah, but he held me captive. I wasn't too touchy-feely with him."

Bjarke's face blanked. He looked at Hector. "My cousin was it?"

Hector nodded briefly and looked to Zaria. "Olaf is up to no good. I told you how he held a boy captive to get Queen Helena's daughter to complete a quest for him."

Zaria looked quickly out to the water, knowing Bjarke would turn to stare at her. She didn't want to be inspected and didn't want to say anything either. She was sure she didn't stand up to the expectations that were held for her. She'd let Hector down. And she'd let herself down when she unwittingly aided Olaf in abducting Hart.

As she glanced down at the water, Zaria saw something strange. A flicker of movement swept along her image. It contorted her features and Zaria felt her heart rate increase. What was that? It looked like a troll in the water. She blinked and leaned over trying to peer beneath the surface of the waves.

Chapter Three:
Circumnavigating Norway

"Oy!" Bjarke cried out, startling her. The image in the water disappeared. Bjarke cried out again as the tender coasted next to the larger ship. "A little help would be appreciated."

Several heads popped over the rail, a mixture of elves and ellefolken. The ellefolken were easily distinguishable from the elves as they were all females with blonde hair and had short tree-like branches growing from their heads. The elves all wore their hair and clothes like they just stepped out of a

Victorian fashion plate, although the females wore split skirts rather than the full skirts of their counterparts in Álfheim.

With the aid of a few of the men they climbed onboard *Ursula*. Aleks and Geirr took off immediately to explore. Every now and then Zaria could hear one of them exclaim about something. Christoffer was looking a bit barmy as he gaped at the ellefolken. He started to ask all kinds of questions of the nearby ladies with a focus on their antlers, which also captured Filip's attention.

Zaria stood patiently next to Bjarke and Hector as they discussed the finer points of the trip ahead. She took everything in from the way the sails rippled in the wind, to the expressions of the crew, to the rigging, and to the hatchways leading toward the cabins.

"They have moonraker sails!" Aleks exclaimed as he raced back toward Zaria.

"What?" she asked, looking up at the sails.

Aleks pointed to the top sail on the masts and explained, "Moonraker sails are used on ships designed for speed."

"That'll be good," Zaria said pragmatically. "I have a feeling we need to get to Jötunheim quickly."

Hector whistled, gaining their attention. They went over and stood in the shade of an overhang. Bjarke left to bark orders at his crew. Elves scrambled for the masts and climbed them quickly, raising and trimming the sails. The ellefolken raced around checking rigging, winches, cleats, and stays.

Hector cleared his throat to gain their attention. Five sets of eyes refocused on the Stag Lord. "We'll be sailing in a few moments. When you're ready let me know and I will show you our cabins. Keep out of the crew's way. Dinner will be served in a few hours. And don't lean over the railings. We don't want you to go overboard."

"Yes, sir," Christoffer said as the others nodded.

As the ship left the bay and entered into the Skagerrak Straight, they all stood aboveboard to take in the sight of Fredrikstad shrinking in the distance. Aleks rambled along about staysails, jibes, and other nautical terms that Zaria tuned out. The wind was beautiful and Zaria loved the feel of it as it swept along her skin and played with her hair. She enjoyed watching the white froth of their wake as they sped along.

They passed a few ships bobbing gently in the waves. It was like they were anchored, even with their sails fully hoisted. This was the effect of the stargazer. It froze humans in place and stopped all surrounding activity.

Zaria was glad she wasn't frozen with them and wondered how many stargazers existed in the world and how wide-spread their effects could be. Aleks' stargazer seemed to be unusually powerful with a reach beyond the limits of a normal application.

Eventually the quintet grew tired and hungry and headed below deck. Even the thrill of the adventure waned for Christoffer compared to a rumbling stomach. His complaining had them all laughing as they searched out the dining room.

***

On the third morning of their circumnavigation around Norway, Zaria found Hector and Bjarke eating sausages and scrambled eggs in the dining room. She felt lethargic and exhausted from another night of restless sleep. Shuffling into the room, she filled a plate of food from the buffet and joined them.

"You're up early," Hector said, watching her closely. "Is everything all right?"

Zaria shrugged. "Sure."

Hector gave her a long look. "All right then."

She picked at her food, uncomfortable. What could she say? That she was having nightmares over a phantasmal image she saw fleetingly in the water days ago? She would appear silly and foolish. Besides, the image that haunted her was her own distorted face, turned into a troll. Anyone would say that was from the water rippling over her reflection, but it hadn't felt like that to Zaria. It had felt very real.

She thought about that for a minute. If it was real, then was it a ghost? In a world of magic surely there were such things as ghosts, or troll-like beings that weren't trolls, like a phooka. Or maybe that was just silly. She could ask about that and if Hector and Bjarke confirmed that ghosts were real, then she could pose her questions about how to get rid of one.

As she ate, Zaria asked as casually as she could, "Are there such things as ghosts?"

Bjarke shook his head. "Nay," he said succinctly. "Ghosts aren't real."

Seeing Zaria's disappointed look, Hector explained, "You have creatures that humans have classed as ghosts, such as banshees, poltergeists, and will-o'-the-wisps."

Bjarke hummed in agreement as he ate a plate of eggs in a single swallow. "But a dead being returning to haunt a location is pure fantasy."

Zaria gave a pointed look at the troll. "You're one to talk. You're a troll."

Hector frowned at Zaria. "Did you sleep well, Princess?"

Zaria slumped and sighed. "Sorry, Bjarke. I don't mean to be rude. Hector is right, I haven't slept well these past few nights."

"It's all right," Bjarke said, unconcerned. He shoveled several sausages into his mouth and chewed happily. "Everyone has a bad day."

"Are you seeing a – ah – ahem – a ghost?" Hector ventured tentatively.

He was all solicitousness, laying a comforting hand on her shoulder and filling her water jug with more to drink. Zaria shook her head vigorously and copied Bjarke with the sausages. If she couldn't talk maybe Hector would leave her alone.

"What does the ghost look like?" Hector probed.

His voice grated on Zaria, and she couldn't take it anymore. She shoved her plate away in contempt. "There is no ghost," she snapped. "I was just asking. Leave me alone!"

"Princess," Hector said conciliatorily. "It's all right. You can tell –"

Zaria refused to be mollified and flounced away. "I'm going above deck. Don't follow me."

She felt Hector's eyes follow her all the way out the door. Her skin prickled in discomfort. She twitched her shoulders in irritation and stomped up the steps, ducking through the hatchway.

Out in the open air, Zaria took a deep breath and felt herself relax. Securing her hair into a quick braid, she tossed it over her shoulder and went over to the mizzenmast at the stern of the ship and began climbing up to the topgallant portion where she straddled the cross-section.

Aleks' enthusiasm for sailing was evidently rubbing off on her, if she knew these nautical terms. That made her huff a small laugh. It helped to break the spell of anger over her. So ghosts weren't real? Big deal. She didn't want to be dealing with a ghost anyway.

The breeze was stronger up here and Zaria felt like she was flying. Stretching her arms out to enjoy the full sensation, she yelled into the wind. Up here away from the others, Zaria was happier. She didn't feel judged by the crew, by Bjarke, by Hector, or by her friends.

She didn't understand the unwarranted scrutiny. She hadn't been in that bad of a mood these past few days. She was usually very good at hiding a grumpy disposition from early mornings or late evenings spent reading. And isn't being moody a teenage thing anyway?

Zaria didn't know how long she'd been up on the mizzenmast, when Christoffer's face popped up by her knees. She gasped and hugged the cross-section quickly for balance. Christoffer laughed and hoisted himself up beside her.

"Your face was hilarious," he said in a friendly manner. With one arm around the cross-section he leaned back and whooped when the ship plunged beneath them. "What a ride!"

Zaria nodded. She felt the same. She didn't have any seasickness being up this high even with the swaying of the ship, whereas she knew Geirr didn't enjoy it and stayed on the top-deck mid-ship to avoid the worst of the swaying as the ship plunged through the waves.

"Hector said you had a tough night. Care to talk about it?" Christoffer asked.

Zaria looked toward him, ready to fight, but he wasn't looking at her. He was absorbed with the shoreline. She looked below and saw Filip standing at the base of the mast with his back pressed against it. He too was looking over the edge of the boat to the shoreline.

"It's just a recurring bad dream," Zaria said. "It's nothing."

"If you say so," Christoffer said mildly. He looked at her with big brown eyes. "What is the dream about?"

Zaria sighed. "I don't want to talk about it."

She slipped off the cross-section, clambering downward. She focused on her footwork and climbed to the deck. Filip nodded to her and pointed to the shoreline.

"The trees are getting smaller," he said. "We must be nearing the tree line."

She ignored Christoffer when he joined them a minute later. He draped his arms over the railing, but didn't say anything. It was a pointed silence which they both observed.

"Tree line?" Zaria asked Filip eventually, curious.

"It's an imaginary line where trees stop growing," Filip said. "Shrubs are then the biggest topiary around. It's roughly the seventy-degree parallel in Norway. Finnmark here we come!"

"Zaria and I estimated that the giants must be about twenty-two meters tall," Christoffer said, offhandedly. "If there are no trees to hide them, how come they haven't been spotted by humans?"

Filip shook his head. "You got me there. Mountains?"

"Not everywhere in Lapland is mountainous though, right? Like the middle. Isn't that flatter?" Zaria asked, trying to recall the topography she saw on one of her maps. "So what then?"

"I can't wait to meet one," Christoffer said.

"Just as long as you don't ask to touch them," Filip joked, elbowing Christoffer in the side. "That was weird."

Christoffer flushed and said defensively, "You had to have been curious too. Maybe Bjarke's skin is rough like a crocodile's skin or slick like a snake's."

"Next you're going to want to feel up the ellefolken's antlers to see if they compare to a reindeer's," Zaria accused with a laugh, giving Christoffer a friendly push.

Her laughter drew the attention of nearby ellefolken which made Christoffer blush a fiercer shade of red. Filip and Zaria exchanged glances and laughed even harder. Zaria felt the lightest she had in days and her moodiness evaporated from one moment to the next. She had needed this.

"Okay, okay, knock it off," Christoffer grumbled.

"I bet you fancy one of them," Zaria teased.

He denied it quickly, but Filip saw him gaze at one of the younger females and pounced. The verbal sparring turned into a quick round of fisticuffs as the boys wrestled. Zaria sidled away and joined the women mending netting. When she sat down on an overturned crate, the lady on her right draped her in netting and handed her a needle and fishing line.

"Watch how it is done," she said in a soft brogue and Zaria watched. After a few stitches she returned the needle and thread to Zaria. "I'm Nora," she added.

"Hello," Zaria said shyly, as she accepted the needle.

She stabbed clumsily at the netting and generally made a mess of things, but the women were content for her to sit there and struggle with the work as they gossiped.

"May I ask a personal question?" Zaria asked, looking up after a while.

Nora nodded. "Of course, Princess."

"Why do you trust Bjarke?" Zaria had wanted to know this for days, but had been unsure of how to bring it up. It seemed to her that if trolls were tricksters then they couldn't be trusted.

Nora looked to the others and then back to Zaria. "Only a few species are all bad," she said simply. "Most others are shades of gray. They can be selfish and greedy and stubborn and wicked, but also selfless and generous and kind and good."

"Which ones are all bad?"

"Dragons," a young girl with short antlers replied. She had a thin white scar running through her right eyebrow. "They're about as bad as it gets. There is no good in them."

"Hector's told me a little about them, and how your people protect the world by helping to keep the dragons trapped in the Under Realm."

"I remember the last time the corruption began to rot the Golden Kings," said Nora, stitching with concentration.

Zaria looked at her keenly. "The golden glade in Gloomwood Forest?"

"Aye," she said. "It happened a little over two hundred years ago."

Zaria stared in amazement. "You don't look forty let alone two hundred years old."

Nora laughed gaily. "Princess, you put me in a fine fettle." She giggled with the woman to her right and continued with her sewing.

"What happened two hundred years ago?" Zaria asked, curious.

She put her netting down and gazed fondly off to the distance. "Hakon was the Stag Lord then. He was incredibly handsome – brawny, strong of shoulder, large antlers, and muscles upon glorious muscles. He loved to roam all over the territories like Hector."

Her friend, an elf, added, "Although Hakon preferred hunting and sport to trading."

"Right," Nora said, gathering the conversation and netting again. "Hakon did not want to be tied down. All the ladies loved him, and he them. He was the biggest of flirts until he sired Hector and settled down."

"You are aware that the ellefolken only have three males at any time in the population?" the girl on Zaria's left said, interrupting.

Zaria nodded, blushing a little. She turned her attention to Nora. "So what happened to Hakon?"

Nora looked at Zaria nonplussed for a moment and then shook her head. "Why nothing. He became reigning king, taking over for his father when the second Golden King became corrupted."

"How does the corruption happen?" Zaria put down the sewing, after stabbing her finger a third time. She was determined not to pick it up again.

"The dragons of course," the girl said. "Me name's Phoebe by the way."

"Nice to meet you," Zaria said automatically, and then added, "but I thought the dragons were imprisoned. How can they corrupt the Golden Kings?"

"Dragons don't like to be imprisoned," Nora said, leaning in conspiratorially.

"I can't imagine anyone does," Zaria replied.

Nora gave her a stern look. "Right, well. Dragons are very powerful, and they are always trying to break out of the Under Realm. Some try to cross the bridge. Some try to swim out. Some try to attack Queen Helena. Some try to break out by attacking the Golden Kings' root system."

"Ellefolken are naturally resistant to rot and corruption just like the alder trees we can turn into," Phoebe boasted. "Some of our kings are twelve hundred years old."

"Alas, some of our kings are swayed by the whispers and promises of the dragons. When they fall, our Stag Lord must join the ranks of the Golden Kings and strengthen the Under Realm's barriers."

Remembering something Hector had said when they first boarded *Ursula*, Zaria leaned in and asked in a whisper. "Does Hakon becoming a Golden King have anything to do with what happened to Bjarke and his river?"

The women all nodded gravely. "Aye," Phoebe said, putting her part of the netting down. "Me mum said that it was Egil, he who inspires fright."

"And Egil is?"

"A dragon. He's one of Koll's younger brothers," Nora explained. "Hakon and Silje figured it out in time, and shut him down. It was a near thing. Next to Koll, Egil is the most dangerous dragon."

"We learn about the dragons through a nursery rhyme," Phoebe said. "Me mother sang it to me to keep me alert to the danger of letting me guard down." She began to hum, and the others joined her in the sea shanty.

In the beginning all was truth and good,
Where it was, there divine light stood.

But then mist covered the ground,
And out of it was darkness found.
It spoilt truth, so it was misunderstood.

What next came from eternal night,
Was born in shadows and inspired fright.
Where fear hides, peace is stolen up and bound,
And good is seemingly lost, never to be found.

But when you see past the delusion,
And know good reigning as the only conclusion,
Away will melt all confusion,
And you will be truth and glory crowned,
Believing not the lies beneath the dragons' hood.

The crew on deck broke into applause to which the ellefolken women bowed their heads, acknowledging the praise. Zaria clapped her hands too, but inside her mind was racing, and her heart beat fast. The song's words felt like they were meant just for her as a warning.

Across the ship her eyes met the boys' gazes. There they stood, all four, equally stunned by the ethereal quality of the ladies' voices. Did they too hear the warning that Zaria heard?

She looked for Hector and saw him standing grimly against the main mast. Bjarke was beside him, his kind round face haunted. Zaria excused herself and made her way to Hector and Bjarke. She had to know more.

Before she could reach either one the ship was surrounded by a pod of humpback whales. This excited the crew, her friends, and frankly Zaria herself. They watched in delight as the whales came to the surface for breath. When a tail flipped and she saw a strange bright blue marking, Zaria asked the elves standing nearby what it was.

A burly man with large forearms squinted and waited to see what she had. When the tail waved again he laughed. "They are under the giants' protection, specifically under the protection of Oskar the Elevated."

"But why mark them blue?"

"To warn goblins and trolls away from hunting them. Giants are very particular about their animals. Each one has a purpose."

"What is the purpose of the whales?" asked Zaria, watching the whales come to the surface of the water. She gasped and ran to the railing. "Oh look a baby!"

The man scratched his jawline. "I believe giants use whales for fishing. Hey – Arty, the whales, why do the giants cultivate them?"

Arty dropped from above and landed lightly on his feet. He looked at the whales, then at Zaria and the man. "Fishing. The whales are like sheepdogs herding fish into the fjords for the giants to gather."

"Seems a bit like fishing from a barrel," Zaria said, frowning. "What about overfishing?"

Arty and the other elf laughed. "Compared to humans overfishing? Do not worry yerself, Princess. The giants know what they are doing."

"Wouldn't humans have noticed the blue markings on the humpbacks?" she asked. "It seems odd, doesn't it?"

"The paint is a spell from the witch in the woods. Humans can't see these animals unless they are onboard a ship like ours or granted permission from a giant."

"A ship like *Ursula*?"

Arty picked up a heavy sack and tossed it over his shoulder. "Owned by a river-troll. Water is kind of their domain, ye can't hide anything from them, if they control the waterway."

"Oh."

"Zaria!" Aleks said running up to her, his freckled face shiny with excitement. "We're going to be pulling into the giant's harbor shortly. They sent the whales to shepherd us to them. Isn't that cool?"

One of the humpbacks breached the water with a mighty splash. They were covered in the spray. Sputtering and laughing, Zaria and Aleks ran over to Geirr and Filip at the bow of the ship to watch *Ursula* turn into a natural harbor. Christoffer was at the wheel with Bjarke, getting a chance to pilot the ship.

The winds were favorable, and *Ursula* sailed speedily into the opening. Mountains soared on either side of the wide channel. Seabirds called out greetings to them. The whales gently guided them through the depths, and what Zaria was seeing finally clicked in her mind, like a picture coming into focus.

"Do you see them?" she whispered breathlessly. "The giants! They're magnificent. Look!"

Zaria pointed to the mountains themselves. Aleks and Geirr shook their heads, bewildered. But Filip saw them, and his mouth dropped open in astonishment.

"No way!" he said. "No freaking way! They're the mountains."

"Not quite," Zaria corrected. "They just blend in really well. Do you see them, Aleks? Geirr?"

"Where?" Geirr complained. "All I see are mountains."

Zaria stuck her arm right in front of his face and pointed. "Follow my arm and finger, watch very closely. They're not moving very much."

Geirr tracked her finger and stared hard at the mountains. When a pair of eyes opened and blinked at him, he stumbled back in surprise. Aleks saw it too, and he was equally shocked. The giants were massive boulder shapes in the landscape, clearly made of, or camouflaged in, the same rocky material as the mountains.

"Wow," Aleks said. "They're massive. Bigger than us by a lot."

Zaria laughed. "What did you expect? Giants only a few feet taller than us? Did you think they could compete in basketball with our athletes?"

Aleks turned red. "Well no, but I didn't expect giant moving rocks either."

Zaria tightened her oversized scarf and tucked her braid out of the way. Putting her hands in her pockets, she watched with rapt attention as the giants awoke and stood and stretched before coming to the shoreline to greet them.

The crew tossed them lines, which Zaria didn't expect the giants to catch because the ropes look like fishing line compared to the size of their hands, but the giants caught them. Very quickly the ship was hauled toward shore. The speed of their docking was breathtaking and effortless for the giants. The tall ship's size was inconsequential to them, an oversized toy.

The crew scrambled to anchor the ship and take down the sails. Soon she and her friends would be disembarking in Jötunheim and would be one step closer to liberating Hart from Olaf's clutches. And that was something to celebrate.

Chapter Four: Trading at Northerly Latitudes

The elation Zaria felt at leaving the ship to mingle with the giants was abruptly doused. The trollish specter from her nightmares flickered ghoulishly at her, acting as her reflection in the water. She tried to ignore it and wondered why nobody else could see it.

Hector and Bjarke spoke animatedly at the front of the tender, going over plans. Bjarke, keen to leave right away, had no interest in staying the night among the giants. Hector tried to persuade him to stay, but was so far unsuccessful. Beside her, the boys jabbered excitedly about the giants.

Now that they were closer to them, the giants were easier to distinguish from the mountainside. They moved purposefully, with a slowness that belied their liveliness. Every face that greeted them was vibrant and enthused. They were happy to have visitors.

Zaria did not join in either conversation. She felt violated, ill at ease, and on display. The specter did not follow her inclination to stare ahead. Instead it twisted her features into something ugly, and taunted her by creeping out of its seat toward her friends and miming attacking them. She shuddered at the ghastly image and turned her face away, tears burning hotly in her eyes.

What was wrong with her? What was this thing? If ghosts did not exist then how was she seeing this thing... this apparition? At least it was silent when she was awake. At night it said all sorts of troubling things. Zaria angrily brushed the tears away and shoved her hands in her pockets. She would ignore it.

"Welcome friends," one of the giants boomed.

His skin was as deep blue as the water with lines of gray marbled throughout, like veins. It was as if he was made of stone. His craggy face towered above them until he knelt on one knee and scooped their tender out of the water. The whole boat fit snugly in his hand with room left over.

"Hector, you look different," the giant boomed, squinting at them.

Hector ran a hand through his unkempt blond hair in a sheepish manner and tugged at his jacket. "Had to camouflage myself amongst the humans. I miss my cloak. Did you keep it safe for me?"

"Of course. And is this the little princess?" he asked, reaching his other hand out to Zaria.

She reached over the heads of the boys and grabbed the tip of the giant's finger with her whole hand, giving it a firm shake. "Hello, sir."

"Call me, Ingdor the Thunderous," he boomed, setting the boat on the ground. Everyone evacuated quickly.

"Hello, Ingdor," Zaria said politely, accepting Filip's help out of the boat.

"How tall are you, Ingdor?" Christoffer shouted, coming up beside Zaria and eagerly reaching out to shake hands with the giant.

He was like a puppy, Zaria thought sourly. Why was he being so embarrassing, asking all kinds of inappropriate questions of the magical species they encountered? He was so rude! How had she not noticed before how annoying he was?

Zaria looked to Aleks and Filip to see if they were as humiliated by Christoffer's antics as she was. To her disappointment they appeared equally enthralled with the giant and hadn't registered Christoffer's question as bad form. She set her mouth in a stubborn moue.

Ingdor wasn't the least bit offended. "I'm as tall as two humpback whales put end to end."

Christoffer looked confused. He looked at the others and then back at Ingdor. "What is that in meters?"

"What's a meter?" asked the giant, raising a brow.

"What about in feet?"

Ingdor chuckled. "Well, that depends. Are you talking about human feet or giant feet?"

"Er… human."

"No idea," Ingdor replied cheerfully. "I've never been very good at math and giant-to-human conversions are a bit tricky on a good day."

"Ingdor, bring our friends up the mountain. We have prepared a feast!" a female giant roared from overhead.

Zaria looked up and caught the smooth unlined face of a giantess disappearing from view.

"Who's that?" Geirr asked, pointing to the giantess.

"My sister," Ingdor replied, scooping up the group. "Bjarke, please come and enjoy the festivities. Astral will have my hide, if I don't extend a gesture of hospitality."

"Nay," said Bjarke, waving his hand dismissively. He barked an order to his crew to gather the tender from the ground and haul it back to the waterline. "We are behind schedule as it is, running all these extra errands for Hector. Time is money and the clock is ticking."

Ingdor shrugged, and the movement nearly toppled Zaria into Filip, who steadied her. "That will disappoint Astral, but I will share your regrets."

"We good?" Bjarke asked, addressing the question to Hector, as he and his crew hopped into the tender and restarted the motor.

Hector nodded. "Consider the debt paid."

"Express my gratitude to Hakon again for his sacrifice. It saved my life."

"I will," Hector said solemnly. "Fair travels, friend."

"Aye," Bjarke said distractedly, shivering. He wrapped his thick scarf tighter around his neck "Ye too. I think ye will need it. Do ye feel it? There's a watchful presence lurking in the shadows."

Hector shook his head. "No, but I will heed the warning."

Bjarke made a hand motion to his crew. The tender began to move backward. Bjarke shouted, "See that ye do! I want to absent me and the crew from here as soon as possible."

Hector didn't say anything to that. He simply turned away and looked up at Ingdor's craggy face. "Shall we join your sister now?"

Geirr leaned over and whispered to Christoffer and Aleks, "What do you think Bjarke meant by all that?"

They both shrugged and Aleks whispered back, "I don't know, but Hector wasn't fazed. I think we're okay."

Geirr frowned. "I don't like the sound of it."

"Me neither," Zaria said, looking back, watching as Bjarke and his crew hoisted the tender parallel to the ship's top decking and climbed out. "I have a feeling it's dragon related."

As soon as she said the word dragon, a shiver raced down her spine. Zaria tugged one of her braids in front of her and nervously played with the end of it. She did not want to meet whatever it was that might be watching them. Was it her watcher?

"That's not good," Aleks said, his expression darkening.

"No," Zaria agreed. "Not good at all."

***

Oskar the Elevated, ruler of the giant tribe on Seiland Island – the high court of Jötunheim – was not as immense as one would expect from a king of the giants. He was shorter than Ingdor by several meters, perhaps by even a half a whale length. The giant had deep-set eyes and a large brow. To Zaria he looked a bit like a Neanderthal, but much larger, and bluer.

"I would have thought the ruler of the giants would be the tallest," Filip said in an aside to Zaria, when Ingdor had released them to their own devices after the introductions.

Aleks nodded. "I wonder why he's called the Elevated."

"Maybe it's a hierarchy thing," Geirr suggested. "The higher the position in the society the grander the title?"

"Or maybe," Hector said with a laugh, having overheard the friends talking, "Oskar is considered Elevated because he's highly intelligent, a characteristic that is greatly prized by giants. Unlike trolls who favor the larger of their kind to rule, wisdom is the measure of a ruler for giants."

Hector went over to Oskar with Zaria and the others trailing behind him. When Hector bowed his head in polite civility, Zaria quickly copied. The boys did likewise.

"This is Princess Zaria of the Under Realm," Hector announced formally, bringing Zaria forward.

She stumbled along, taken aback by Hector's pronouncement of her title. Until right now it had always seemed more like a nickname than a fact. If Zaria was royalty, she certainly never felt like it. She bobbed a quick curtsey.

"Greetings, Princess," Oskar rumbled like a distant storm. His accent was thick and cultured. Each word uttered was deliberate and unhurried. "Did you bring something to trade?"

Just as Zaria was going to say no, Hector stepped forward and bowed. "Eight months ago when Zaria and I first met, I told her how much the giants loved music. She and her friends were so good as to create new playlists for the Seiland giants. If Oskar can wait patiently for one moment, I will retrieve the iPads from our bags."

"Very well," Oskar said.

Hector left her and the boys to seek out their belongings on the other side of the flat outcropping. Zaria was glad to have something to offer, even if she didn't know what it was she was offering exactly. She hoped Hector had good taste in music.

"Do you play an instrument?" Zaria ventured, casting about for a safe topic.

Oskar gave her a slow blink. "I do not. Even though I am smaller than my brethren, my fingers are still too big for human instruments."

Zaria blushed, embarrassed. "Right. I'm glad we didn't bring you a piano then. That would have been silly."

"Hmm," Oskar replied, noncommittally.

Zaria felt adrift. She looked at the others and Christoffer immediately put himself forward. He bowed to Oskar again and stood.

"Your Majesty," he began.

"Your Elevated," Oskar corrected benignly. "His Majesty is my cousin."

Christoffer nodded. "Your Elevated, I must ask, how do your people get their names?"

For once Zaria didn't mind her friend's blundering ways. Right now, he was saving her bacon with his small-talk.

"We have a register of courtesy titles," Oskar replied. "A baby's name is chosen from this register based on a formula that calculates the month, day, and year of formation. This title is held by the babe for its entire life. The title is only relinquished back into the pool of available names at transformation."

"Transformation? What's that?" he asked.

"We call it transformation when we become one with the rocks."

"Death?" Christoffer guessed.

Aleks hit him on the back of the head. "I think Oskar means that the giants actually transform into rocks."

Oskar smiled, his face splitting and fracturing like bedrock under stress. "Yes. Giants are bound to the land. We form from the bedrock and return to it. Seiland has been the home of our tribe for centuries upon centuries."

"So why do you eat fish?" Filip asked. "Wouldn't you eat rocks?"

Oskar laughed, and his laughter made the earth tremble. He was joined by a giantess of equal years, with long dark curly hair that looked like moss.

"Children," Oskar said, motioning the giantess forward. "This is my wife, Seila the Altitudinous. Seila, this young lady is Princess Zaria, Queen Helena's daughter."

"Actually," Zaria said. "I'm the daughter of Colonel and Meredith Fierce."

Oskar regarded her, his expression grave. "I thought Hector said –"

"I'm adopted," Zaria explained. "Queen Helena is my birth mother, but Merry is my mother. She raised me."

"Ah, Seila," Hector said, rejoining the group. He was wearing his familiar clothes again. His white cloak proudly situated on his shoulders and his antlers high on his head. He bowed deeply to the giantess. "To a lowly observer you are grander and more beautiful than the highest mountain peaks. Allow me to present you and your husband the items the children and I brought to trade."

"You flatter me, Stag Lord," Seila demurred, accepting the parcels Hector handed to her.

She sat next to Oskar on a large carved stone bench. She was a meter or two taller than Oskar seated. Her wide round eyes settled on Zaria.

"We will discuss trading later. First, the little princess objects to us referring to her as Queen Helena's daughter."

Hector glanced in askance to Zaria. She tilted her chin up in response, daring him to question her. He shrugged and looked back at the giants.

"She hasn't seen or heard from Helena in over twelve years," he explained. "It's understandable if she doesn't feel overly familial."

"When does Queen Helena plan to meet her daughter, Stag Lord?" Oskar asked.

Zaria sucked in a breath and stared at Hector, anticipation buzzing in her belly.

"I do not know, your Elevated," Hector replied, instantly destroying Zaria's unspoken hopes. "Correspondence with Helena has been stifled by the recent events with the river-troll and the creeping spread of rot by the Golden Kings."

"Your time of transformation is coming soon," Seila said with compassion. "I know for you it is not something to celebrate, but you will be at one with nature again."

"Yes, your Altitudinous," Hector replied stoically.

"Our cousins in Stabbursdalen are facing difficulties with the allies of Olaf of the Glomma," Oskar confided. "They seek our assistance."

Hector nodded. "He is recruiting from Gloomwood Forest and sending his lackeys to harass the former allies from the Dragomir Wars – the giants, elves, and ellefolken. Even the mountain-trolls of Trolgar are being targeted by Olaf, although their alliance with the river-troll was uneasy to begin with."

"We must keep an eye on King Kafirr. I do not trust him to honor his word," Oskar said.

Seila rested her hand comfortingly on his arm. "I agree," she said. "King Kaffir's vacillation is well known. He changes with the wind. Remember how he, his pa, and his people swapped sides thrice in the Dragomir Wars?"

"Silje is watching him. She has sent skilled diplomats and swordsmen to keep Kafirr firmly checked. He can be a great asset."

"Wait –" Zaria interjected, her head spinning with all this new information. "So, you're saying Olaf is recruiting others to stir up problems?" Hector and the giants nodded. "Is this so we're caught off guard when Koll's released?" Zaria asked.

"Yes, Princess," Seila said, "and right now, an awful nest of hags have settled in Stabbursdalen. Their wolverines are killing local wild life and preying on the auroch herds."

"Aurochs are cattle. They're bigger than your cows," Hector explained at Zaria's blank look.

Oskar touched Seila's arm. "Don't forget about the missing tourists in the Varanger Peninsula." He looked at Hector. "We suspect that they've been killed by banshees."

"What is being done to stop Olaf and his allies?" Aleks demanded. "Attacks on tourists are going to be noticed."

Oskar inclined his head. "We are handling it. We've sent emissaries to Rjupa the Bountiful and to Petronella the Measureless."

Aleks looked disgusted. He muttered under his breath to Geirr, "Politics. When does it ever get anything done?"

***

Late in the evening, hours after the feast that had been prepared by Ingdor's sister, Zaria and her friends were full and couldn't eat another bite. They sat around a large hole, dug deep into the mountain. Inside the hole a bonfire crackled, its flames licking the surface.

Although it had been only a few hours, it was easy to tell that Astral the Celestial and her brother were the least conservative of the giants they'd met. Both talked animatedly, whereas their other dinner partners measured their words even more carefully than Oskar and Seila.

With Lohcca the Whale, Ello the Empyrean, and Rikkar the Achiever, Zaria quickly learned that the long silence that stretched out after a question was not because the giants hadn't heard her ask, but was the result of a full deliberation in order to provide the best answer.

Christoffer and Geirr still hadn't caught on, which had Zaria and Aleks rolling in silent laughter as Geirr tried to speed up responses by talking louder. He was practically shouting now to Ello, an old giantess with a face so wrinkly and skin so translucent it looked like tissue paper plastered wetly to a stone surface.

Zaria could only guess that Geirr thought her hard of hearing, because she looked so ancient. Next to him, Christoffer was pantomiming everything to get his point across to Rikkar who would clap his hands in delight after every gesture, but failed to respond audibly. It was obvious that the boys were getting frustrated.

"Guys," Filip said, interjecting into Geirr's fourth explanation of a question. "Ello understands you. She chooses not to answer immediately, so she can think over her response before giving it. Let her think."

Christoffer stared at Filip aghast. Aleks burst out laughing at his friend's flummoxed expression.

"You should see the look on your face," he chortled, clutching at his sides. "You look like somebody hit you in the face with a bat."

"Do you mean to say –" Geirr started, and then stopped. His mouth hung open like a fish. He looked up at Ello. "You knew what I meant all along?" He sounded stung.

Zaria's lips twitched. She hid her laughter behind her hand. "Yes," Zaria replied, snickering. "She did."

Ello nodded gently and Rikkar inclined his head. Christoffer and Geirr turned red in embarrassment. They mumbled apologies and fidgeted, uncomfortable now in Ello's and Rikkar's presence.

Hector approached and drew Zaria aside. She followed him across the wide clearing to where Oskar and Seila sat comfortably on the ground, sunlight glinting off their faces. It sounded odd to think about sunlight at night, but this far north at this time of year, the sun hung in the sky refusing to dip below the horizon. The angle of it cast the world in a strange orange and purple twilight.

The giantess stroked the head of a creature in her lap. Zaria was floored to recognize it was a woolly mammoth. Seila treated it like a pet dog. The mammoth was leaning into the giantess' caress and wagging its tail. Zaria wondered if there were any more Ice Age critters around, and she craned her head to look.

"Princess Zaria," Seila greeted, her round face composed and genteel.

Zaria stopped looking around and bobbed a quick curtsy. "Your Altitudinous; your Elevated."

"My husband and I have listened to a sampling of your music. It's quite –" she turned to Oskar, "What is the word I am searching for, dear?"

"Energetic," Oskar offered.

Seila nodded. "Energetic is a good word. Yes, the music was energetic and bright. Very happy, I feel."

"Was the music new to you?" Zaria asked.

"It was," Oskar replied. "What would you like from us for it?"

"For the pop music," Hector said, subtly sharing with Zaria what was on the iPads, "we would like to trade passage to Vadsø and an introduction to the dwarvish courts of Jerndor."

"That would involve getting help from Petronella the Measureless and her giants. I would have to trade with her to enlist her aid and that would cut into our bounty."

"I can provide the trade to Petronella," Hector replied. "It would cost you nothing."

"Will you be trading to her the same music you have traded to us or different music?"

Hector fingered his beard and studied Oskar carefully. Zaria thought perhaps he was trying to take Oskar's measure. It was a good thing he didn't have to do that with her Measurelessness. It would be impossible if you trusted Petronella's title. Zaria snickered to herself. Hector shot her a quelling look, which made her giggle more.

"Oskar," Hector began, "we have traded for many moons. I have brought you precious stones, music, human equipment, and magic. I would not give Petronella something that I have not already given you. Your court will still be greater than hers."

Oskar shared a long look with his wife. The conversation between them was entirely silent, but when they turned back to Hector and Zaria the rulers were on the same page. Seila put down her woolly mammoth and reached out to Zaria.

"Climb aboard," she said.

Zaria grabbed the giantess' thumb and was hauled up into the air. She was suddenly at equal height with the giantess, staring her straight in the eyes.

"You are a curious thing, Zaria Fierce," Seila stated.

She pinched Zaria's arm and lifted it up and down. Zaria felt like a rag doll. She tried to break her arm free, but it wasn't until the giantess let her loose that Zaria reclaimed the limb.

"How am I curious?" Zaria queried, feeling a little cross at the manhandling.

"You're such a tiny thing and yet big things happen because of you. How do you explain this?"

Zaria clasped her hands behind her back and rubbed one shoe against her other foot. "Dragons are involved. It was always going to be a big adventure."

Seila considered this, and then said, "My grand-mère was there when Koll was first captured five hundred years ago. He was the last dragon caught. Before my grand-mère transformed, she told me that Koll wouldn't rest until he was free again to terrorize the world and to cover it in darkness. This sword you seek can free him, just as easily as it captured him."

Zaria gulped. "Then, it's imperative it doesn't fall into the hands of Olaf or his allies."

"Yes, but can you keep it safe?"

Hector cleared his throat. Zaria lost her footing when the giantess moved her hand. Seila peered down at Hector, oblivious to Zaria clinging tightly from her thumb.

"You have something to say, Stag Lord?"

"Zaria is meeting with the high court of the dwarves to prove she's Helena's heir. They were charged to guard it until she was of age to claim it. They take that vow seriously; they would not even let me inside their kingdom for fear I was there to steal it."

"It is too much power in the hands of someone so small. I object to this scheme of yours. I understand your peoples are much plagued by Olaf and that you cannot properly perform your duties until your son is restored, but I do not see how this sword will free him. It is much too dangerous to pursue."

Hector folded his arms and stared hard at the giantess. "It is a risk. Olaf could be setting a trap to seize the sword, but I must possess the sword to free my Hart from his chains. Olaf tied him up the same way we tied up the dragons, with chains given to him by the dwarves of Malmdor."

Seila glanced at Oskar and again their gazes seemed to pass along a whole conversation. Zaria climbed unsteadily to her feet and looked between the two, anger growing in her heart.

Oskar cleared his throat uneasily as he fingered the bag of goods Hector had provided for the trade. The giant wanted the music it was plain to see, but he hesitated.

"It is a pity," he finally said, handing over the bag, "but I'm afraid we cannot trade."

Hector made an angry noise. "My son is innocent. He does not deserve to be imprisoned."

Oskar nodded sadly. "A terrible pity, but my hands are tied, Stag Lord."

Zaria pressed her lips together, letting anger wash over her. She stamped her foot. "If you do not help, we will find a way to reach the dwarves. Hart deserves his freedom. He would not be in the predicament he's in, if it weren't for me. I can't *not* help him."

Hector grunted. "She's right. I managed to reach their doorstep once. If I have to guide the children through those same dangers, it will be slow going, for the way is perilous. Do not make me take these children through the fey courts."

"We are grieved to wound you, Stag Lord," Oskar said, sounding indeed grieved, but he continued firmly, "but the Seiland giants of Jötunheim cannot and will not help you in this request. The safety of all is more important than the freedom of one."

Chapter Five: Help from Unexpected Heights

Hector woke Zaria and her friends in the middle of the night. The midnight sun cast their surroundings in a strange blanket of gray and orange, where light and shadow met and mingled. He pressed a finger to his lips to indicate they should be silent and then motioned for them to collect their things.

Zaria, bleary-eyed and confused, was more than happy to be pulled out of her recurrent nightmare. She hated more than anything being trapped inside a dream and being unable to rouse herself out of it.

Filip helped her gather her things and slung them over his shoulder. Zaria protested, but was silenced by a pointed look from Filip.

"I got this," he whispered, nudging her shoulder with his. "You can have it back after you wake-up, Zar-Zar."

She made a face, but fell in line as Hector gathered them together and pointed over to the trail leading down the mountainside.

"We must go," he said cryptically and started walking.

Geirr yawned widely and straightened his collared shirt, tucking it into his dark blue jeans. Zaria shook her head bemused. Even on a trip across the country, Geirr still tried to look neat and tidy. At least his clothes were slightly wrinkled from being tossed into his backpack. If he'd brought an iron, she wouldn't have been able to resist teasing him.

Aleks and Filip were not nearly as smartly dressed. Both wore T-shirts, shorts, and sneakers that had seen better days. Christoffer was hopeless; his clothes were half-on and half-off, as he hopped up and down on one foot to put on first one hiking boot and then the other.

Zaria was somewhere between cute and casual. She wore black leggings under a blue tunic top with a well-worn jacket thrown on for warmth. Her feet were laced up in dirty black and white canvas sneakers. Her hair was braided as usual, but her braids had started to frizz. She pulled them back into a loose ponytail off her face.

Hector was wearing his trademark hooded white cloak with his golden antlers perched on top of his head. He moved swiftly and silently over the terrain, navigating the barely marked path with ease. The four friends trailed sleepily behind him, as he took them down the mountain.

The part of the path they were on now wasn't very steep, but Zaria still had to lean backwards with each step so as not to trip if she went too fast. Aleks pulled out packets of granola and some kind of squeezable fruit-mix and passed them out. Zaria took hers gratefully and munched on the granola bar as she enjoyed the peekaboo views of the sea through the trees.

"Where are we going?" Aleks asked when he finished his squeezable, stuffing the trash into his pocket.

"We still need to be quiet," Hector replied, waving them ahead of him. "The sun will rise higher soon and wake the giants. Then it will be too late for us to get away from Seiland undetected."

When Zaria drew even with Hector, he slowed down and kept pace with her. As they walked, he rooted inside his bag and handed her a folded paper. Curious, she unfolded it and stared at it with growing excitement.

It was a map! She loved maps, especially antique ones. This was not just any old map though; it was a map of Norway with the whole country broken down into the different magical kingdoms.

She scanned it in awe, touching the crinkled vellum with reverence. To see how the kingdoms overlapped fascinated her. Giants, dwarves, humans, elves, ellefolken, and fey all shared space together. And humans had no idea!

Jötunheim was broken down into five giant factions, some of which spilled across Sweden and Finland. In the top left of the country was Seiland, their current location. Oskar the Elevated was handwritten under Seiland. Rjupa the Bountiful and Petronella the Measureless were written under the Varanger Peninsula with question marks. She pointed it out to Hector.

He shrugged and whispered, "I don't know how the region is split between the giantesses and their clans."

Zaria returned to the map. The top right showed the human city of Vadsø and the dwarves' empire of Jerndor nearby. She wondered how that worked, but would wait to ask.

Hector had marked a route which took them through the fey country of Niffleheim. The boundary for Niffleheim was less distinct in the west than in the east. Perhaps there wasn't a natural boundary or maybe Hector didn't know where the fey defined their boundaries.

Hector tapped her on the shoulder. He pointed to the Glomma, drawing her attention to a tributary that ran almost horizontally to it. He pointed to a name in the margins.

Bjarke.

"His river?" she whispered. Now Bjarke's comment about Olaf as his cousin made sense. Their rivers connected.

Hector nodded, took the map back, and refolded it carefully. He tucked it inside his bag and hefted the bag over his shoulder. With a finger he pointed to the shoreline, which was finally visible to the group.

Zaria saw Ingdor and Astral half submerged in the water. Astral had her hair pulled back in a tight ponytail. Ingdor wore a swim cap. They looked grim. Hector greeted them quietly, his greeting was acknowledged silently.

Hector beckoned Zaria and the boys closer and closer again. When they were huddled around him, Hector leaned in, his antlers almost knocking into Geirr.

Quick reflexes saved Geirr from losing an eye, as Hector caught him before he stumbled backward.

"We're leaving," Hector said, nodding subtly toward the giants. "Ingdor and Astral have agreed to take us to the boundaries of Niffleheim. This is a great boon to us, but we must continue to be silent. If Oskar were to hear us, he would stop them. Understood?"

Christoffer looked at the others and back to Hector. "Uh… no."

Aleks shook his head. "No, but we can keep quiet. You can explain later."

"Good," Hector whispered. "Zaria, Filip, and I will go with Astral. Aleks, Geirr, Christoffer you will go with Ingdor. Remember, stay silent."

The group broke apart with Geirr taking the lead. He walked over to Ingdor who offered him a hand to climb aboard. At Hector's urging, Zaria and Filip went over to Astral. She didn't offer a hand. Instead, she grabbed them and placed them on her head.

Zaria stifled a yelp as she and Filip fell into each other. Hector hushed her, righting them both swiftly. Their feet touched on the top of Astral's ponytail holder. Hector then gave them each a length of rope and showed them how to tie themselves into Astral's hair.

To Zaria, Astral's hair felt like a pumice stone. It was pale, rough, and porous. She wondered why the rope was needed, because Astral's hair wasn't slippery at all. She shared a glance with Filip and copied Hector, securing herself to Astral's hair.

Nearby the others were sitting on Ingdor's shoulders. Christoffer was grinning hugely and swinging his feet. Zaria shared a look with Filip and rolled her eyes. Aleks reached out to smack Christoffer lightly upside the head when he flailed and pretended to slip off Ingdor's shoulder.

Hector tugged on Astral's locks and gave a hand signal to Ingdor. The sibling giants turned and stepped farther out into the Norwegian Sea. As they walked they were careful to not raise their feet above the waterline. Even with their precautions, the waves splashed and slapped noisily against them. The water rose until both giants were almost fully submerged.

Zaria was grateful for the rope securing her to the giantess' hair. Some of Astral's movements were so jerky and uncoordinated that had Zaria not been tied into place she would have tumbled off and into the cold sea below.

"Do you think they'll swim?" Filip whispered, nudging Zaria.

At Hector's glare, she kept quiet and nodded. The water had to be deep, even for a giant. Zaria leaned around the giantess' head to watch the distant shoreline. They would be on the mainland soon. Zaria figured ten to fifteen minutes. Surely once they arrived there, Hector would lift the ban on speaking.

Water plumed in the air to her left, close to Ingdor and the others. Zaria gasped. The humpback whales were back. Ingdor surged forward to keep away from the pod.

Astral hummed anxiously at their presence, as the whales swam closer to them. She tilted forward, stroking quickly through the water. The movement forced Zaria deep into Astral's stony hair and she scraped her elbow unpleasantly.

Hector put a protecting arm across both of the children's backs and tugged the giantess' hair. In the distance a loud bellow cried out from the mountains. It reached them like a hurricane.

Hector cursed and yelled, "No point in subtlety now, we must get to the mainland."

"The whales are too close," Astral replied. Indeed one was swimming alongside her and nudged them occasionally. "I won't hurt them."

Hector said nothing, but looked back over his shoulder. Zaria did too and was surprised to see the trees move and shake.

"Oskar has sent giants to capture us to keep us from going northward."

"Why is he so set against us leaving?" Filip asked, frowning as the advancing giants broke through the tree line and waded into the water.

Hector sighed. When he spoke, his words were full of regret. "The Seiland giants, indeed most of the tribes of Jötunheim, but the Seiland giants in particular, lost more than half of their population in the Dragomir Wars."

Astral spoke, spitting out a mouthful of water. "We giants value freedom and liberty. It is not a principle we can sacrifice at the changing of the winds. Oskar will come to his senses. Then he will be grateful for our actions."

"We hope," Ingdor added darkly, and glanced over his shoulder, which nearly upset the trio riding there.

"Hey!" Christoffer complained loudly. "Don't knock us off!"

"Oops," Ingdor said, "Sorry."

At this point, Astral and Ingdor were about halfway to the other side of the channel, but the giants following them had closed that distance by half. The whales crowding them slowed the siblings' progress tremendously. The brother and sister refused to get rough with the whales.

To Zaria, it seemed as if the whales were winning and pushing them backwards. She watched closely and discovered she wasn't imagining it. The whales were trying to herd the siblings backwards. Back toward Seiland!

"What do we do about the whales?" she asked, worried.

"Nothing," Ingdor said. "They're too precious."

Ingdor caught one of the humpback whales and tucked it under his arm like an American football or a woman's purse. It squirmed and squawked. At least it sounded like a squawk. Ingdor rubbed its nose briefly before reaching out to gently push another humpback away. Astral too was fending off the pod from all sides.

"Halt!" called a deep slumberous voice.

Zaria looked over her shoulder and saw the pursuing giants within a few whale lengths of them.

Her pulse leapt. "Hector, we're not going to make it."

Hector eyed the distance to the far shore and the closeness of the lead giant behind them. "No," he agreed.

"I'm going to toss you," Astral warned as she pushed three overly friendly humpbacks away.

They slapped their tails loudly on the surface of the water. She smacked the water with her hands, echoing the sound. It wasn't a game, it meant something, but Zaria couldn't tell what.

"Toss us?" A grin spread across Filip's face. "Yes!"

"No time like the present," Ingdor agreed.

In a short span of breaths, Zaria, Hector, and Filip were plucked up by the giantess and with a breathless scream she threw them over the whale pod. Zaria hated the sensation. Her stomach tight with the anticipation of hitting the water, Zaria cringed at the fast approaching waves.

The boys thrilled at being thrown. They whooped and yelled with the exhilaration of it. What she wouldn't give for Norwick at this moment.

"Cannonball," Christoffer yelled, seconds before impact, assuming the shape he called out.

Zaria didn't hesitate; she copied and saw the others do the same. Even Hector tucked in and with a series of mighty splashes they hit the water, sinking fast into the chilly deep.

She gasped for air as she broke the surface of the water. Whirling around, she looked for the others. Hector's hood had fallen down the back of his cloak, and he looked as happy as a wet cat – which is to say not at all. He swam to Zaria.

Filip and Geirr broke the surface next. Both spat out water and began treading to keep afloat. Grins spread across their faces and they high-fived each other.

"Awesome," Filip said.

Aleks popped up between them. He wiped water out of his eyes and tossed his head, wiping his hair off his forehead. He splashed the others and ducked at their retaliation.

When he resurfaced, he said, "I don't know about anyone else, but I'm ready for a campfire and s'mores now."

"Or a hot bath," Zaria agreed. "Where's Christoffer?"

Hector looked down and around, but it was impossible to see through the glare on the water.

"Hold on," he muttered, and then took a deep breath and dove under the surface.

Zaria and Aleks looked around anxiously.

"Christoffer!" Aleks called. "Christoffer!"

Filip and Geirr called out too as Hector resurfaced. The Stag Lord spat out a mouthful of water and wiped water from his eyes, hair, and beard. He rapped Aleks on the head to get his attention.

"Your friend is over there," he told the boys, pointing toward the shoreline.

Christoffer was climbing from the waves onto the sandy beach. He turned around and waved at them.

"He's safe. Let's go," Hector said, swimming away.

Zaria looked over her shoulder and saw Ingdor and Astral surrounded by the other giants. The whales encircled the group, spraying water through their blowholes. She hoped their giant friends would be okay and that Oskar wouldn't punish them.

Filip splashed her. "Come on Zar-Zar, let's get out of the water."

She nodded and they bodysurfed to the shore. When they reached it, Christoffer offered her a hand and hauled her out of the water. Her clothes made sucking noises as they clung to the waves. She came free with a wet *slurp* and stumbled into Christoffer. He caught her and righted them both to keep them from falling onto the sand.

Water ran down in rivulets off Hector's cloak, the hood dragged low with the weight of the water. With as much dignity as he could muster, he trudged up the beach to the grassy knoll. Aleks and Geirr stumbled along together behind him, sand clinging to their shoes, legs, and clothes.

Zaria wiggled her toes in her canvas sneakers feeling how waterlogged they were. She did not relish traipsing all over Norway in them. She could easily picture wrinkly toes and the musty smell that would accompany peeling off her socks.

Hector tossed his soaked bag onto the ground, followed it with his dripping cloak, and wrung out his beard. "All right, gather up."

Zaria looked back at the water. Their giant friends were almost back at Seiland Island, herded by the other giants and the whales. The whales began to hang back, staying in the deeper waters.

"Will Astral and Ingdor be okay?" she asked.

Hector frowned, following Zaria's gaze. "Oskar will come around. We simply didn't have time to argue with him. Time is of the essence. We must get the sword and free Hart."

"Why did we have to sneak away?" Christoffer asked. He shook his head like a dog, spraying the group with water.

"Ew," Zaria said. "Stop that."

Christoffer laughed and flicked more water at her. His black hair stood at attention, sleek and spikey. She glared at him. She was not amused.

Hector sighed. "He's a ponderer, less set in his ways than the elders, but more inclined to wait and overanalyze a decision than the younger giants. It seems to be their way."

Hector dropped to one knee and began rummaging through his bag. He pulled out the iPads, chargers, wireless speakers, and other gadgets and dumped them on the ground.

Christoffer and Geirr exchanged looks. Geirr cleared his throat and said, "Okay, so Oskar ponders. That doesn't really explain sneaking off in the twilight hours."

"It's all ruined," Hector said, disgusted. He dropped the saturated gadgets and kept digging through his bag. "I know you're here somewhere, where are you?"

"Oskar the ponderer," Christoffer prodded.

"Hm?" Hector asked, distracted. "Oh right. Oskar knew our plans and didn't approve. He would not have supported us on the journey ahead and would have delayed us by every means necessary. Namely, as is the giant way, one cannot leave their home – or kingdom – without making a trade."

"And he rejected our trade," Zaria added, understanding now, "but we could not have traded for less, because of Hart."

"Exactly," Hector agreed. He reached so far into the bag – it was like his shoulder disappeared. Zaria blinked. "Gotcha," he crowed and pulled his arm out of the bag.

Zaria and the others leaned in closer to see. Hector cupped the object with both hands blocking their view of whatever it was. At the sight of a small fist pushing Hector's fingers aside, Zaria jumped.

"What is that?" Aleks asked, leaning closer to look.

Hector revealed the creature.

"Master Brown," Filip exclaimed, surprised to see the brownie they had met on their last adventure.

"Madam Brown," the creature retorted shrilly.

When Zaria looked closer, it was obvious that the creature was a shorter female counterpart to Master Brown, which was saying a lot, because he'd been fairly short to begin with. She had the same blue skin and beady eyes, but her face was rounder and kinder than Master Brown's.

"We're so sorry, Madam Brown. How is your husband?" Geirr asked.

"Who are you talking about?" she demanded, crossing her arms. Her glare was ferocious. "I tis not married."

Hector smiled. "Madam Brown, the children aren't knowledgeable about brownies. They do not know your title signifies your experience in caregiving. In the human world your name and honorific mean you are married."

"So does this mean they're all Master Browns and Madam Browns?" Aleks whispered to Zaria and Geirr. She shrugged.

Geirr whispered back, "She was in his bag. Doesn't anyone find that odd?"

Hector turned toward the children. "Madam Brown is a highly skilled caregiver and far more than I deserve."

Madam Brown blushed, and the blush turned her skin purple. "Tis an honor," she cooed, throwing her apron over her face and giggling.

"I found Madam Brown acting as custodian for an abandoned farm. She did such a good job that most humans didn't realize it stood empty. I traded with her for years and have been impressed with her."

"Stag Lord, tis too much," Madam Brown said, giggling into her apron. "No more. Please."

Hector nodded, forgoing further compliments. "When Hart was kidnapped," he explained, "I begged her to join me as I searched for him, knowing that he would need her expertise when he was found."

Madam Brown dropped her apron. She gazed at Hector fondly and said with all earnestness, "You will find your Hart."

"Thank you," he said. "Now, Madam Brown, I'm sure you've noticed, but we are in a bit of a pickle. Our giant friends tossed us into the sea and now everything we own is wet and most likely ruined. Can you work your magic to fix what things you can for us?"

That's when Zaria noticed that Madam Brown was dry and clean. She'd skipped over this observation earlier during the introductions. It would make more sense for the brownie to be drenched like the rest of them, but she wasn't.

"I've just been waiting for you to ask," she said.

Abruptly she changed shape, growing a foot taller. Now Madam Brown matched Master Brown's height. Christoffer did a double-take. Zaria was fairly certain she had as well. It simply wasn't something one sees every day.

"She comes in two sizes," Geirr muttered. "Regular and travel size."

Aleks and Filip snickered, which caught Madam Brown's attention. They sobered under her beady regard. Then she clucked at the boys and waved her hands at them.

A wind blew over them, leaving their hair sticking straight-up. The sand on their shoes, legs, and clothes was gone. Their clothes and hair dry. The wind had reddened their cheeks slightly and left them looking slightly stunned.

Zaria hid a smile behind her hand. Like with the boys, an intense wind blew over her. It was very warm. She imagined it was like standing under the dryers of an automated car wash. Her cheeks flapped slightly, pulling back from her teeth.

When it was done, Zaria checked herself over. She was clean and dry, although she could tell by touching her hair that her braids had seriously frizzed. She started undoing them. After she fixed her braids, she looked over the rest of the group.

Christoffer thought the experience cracking good fun and was pestering Madam Brown for information on how she did it. Geirr looked calm and collected – smartly dressed as ever. He even looked a little pressed, although there were still a few stubborn wrinkles. Hector looked… well, he looked fuzzy. It made her giggle. The fur on his cloak went every which way similar to a frazzled cartoon cat. He was using a brush to smooth it back down.

Madam Brown was holding and examining the devices Hector had dropped on the ground. She muttered under her breath and zapped one with short bursts of electricity. She prodded and poked and peered into sockets.

Zaria looked for her backpack, located it next to Aleks' and picked it up. Like them, her bag was dry from the brownie's magic. Zaria murmured her appreciation and briefly rummaged inside before pulling out one of her maps and smoothing it out.

The map was water damaged. The text and graphics in the creases were blurred and bleeding. The map itself was fragile, threatening to tear at the slightest hint of rough handling. Zaria was almost afraid to stretch it out all the way.

Geirr settled himself next to her on the ground and looked at the map with her. He pointed to their approximate location. Zaria nodded.

"I'm going to mark the map," she explained, reaching into her bag and pulling out a permanent marker. "Hector," she called out, looking over at him.

"Yes, Princess?"

"May I borrow your map, please? I would like to copy your notes."

Hector reached into his bag and pulled out the map. He handed it to her. As she unfolded it, she felt it tear. Zaria cringed, before proceeding with caution, opening the map more slowly. When it was fully open, Zaria sighed in frustration. The ink had bled off completely. There was nothing left delineating the boundaries of the magical communities.

"It's gone," she said, holding the map out to Hector to take.

He glanced at it and scratched his beard. "That's unfortunate. Luckily, you five have me. I remember the way." He tapped his temple.

"It would have been nice to have," Zaria said with obvious frustration. "Can you mend it, Madam Brown?"

The brownie shook her head. "'Tis not under my control."

"What?"

"'Tis not under my control," she squeaked defensively, crossing her arms to glare at Zaria.

"She can't read," Hector whispered softly. "She can't fix what she doesn't know. I'm afraid the electronics might be shot too, but I haven't the heart to tell her."

The brownie's ears turned purple in embarrassment, but she pretended not to hear and so Zaria pretended not to know.

Chapter Six: At the Bottom of a Well

"Should we get moving?" Aleks questioned, glancing up at the sky.

Hector glanced up and around. He rubbed the back of his neck, put his hood up, and slung his bag over his shoulder. "Yes, we should. Access to the Niffleheim isn't far."

"What is the Sniffle-heim?" Geirr asked.

"Niffleheim," Hector corrected.

"Bless you," Christoffer said, laughing loudly at his own joke.

Zaria rolled her eyes. "It's fey country."

Aleks looked at Hector in askance, the freckles on his face standing out against his sudden pallor. "Fey country?" he croaked.

Hector nodded. "Stay brave, lad. It'll be okay. Hopefully we won't meet anyone. The fey retreated long ago at the end of the Dragomir Wars, and hid themselves away. They don't want any part of this, I am certain."

Aleks bit his lip, his expression pensive. He didn't say anything. Zaria went over to him and gave him a hug. He responded sluggishly, clearly upset about traveling into the heart of the fairy courts.

"It'll be okay," she whispered. "Even if we meet any fairies, they probably won't be your birth parents. You're safe."

"I really don't want to do this," he told her. "I never cared to meet them. I don't want to meet any of them."

She hugged him again. "Why are you worried?"

"Grams told me to never seek out the fey. She said it was dangerous. She said they hated changelings and did terrible things to any who returned."

Zaria didn't know what to say to that. She wanted to avoid the fey now too with that knowledge. Rescuing Hart would be meaningless, if her friend got hurt along the way.

Hector bent down and took Aleks by the shoulders. "You have my word, I will not let any harm come to you down there."

"We have to go underground?" Aleks protested. He looked wildly at the others. "There has to be another way!"

Hector shook her friend, getting his attention. "I promise you, you'll be safe. You're stronger than you think."

"Why do they hate changelings?" Zaria asked, resting a comforting hand on Aleks' back. "We should know all the facts before we cross into Niffleheim."

The others formed around Aleks and stared at Hector. They stood behind their friend, a tangible wall of protection. Only Madam Brown stood on Hector's side. Hector dropped his hands and stood up, running a hand along the back of his neck.

"Do you want me to tell them, or do you want to share with them what your grandmother told you?"

Aleks didn't say anything. He just scuffed his shoes in the dirt.

Hector looked at the children. "It could be one of three things. First, the fey have very strict standards of beauty. Changelings are fey children who do not meet that standard and are cast out. Sometimes they are swapped for other children – most times now – not. They're simply abandoned."

"Grams said because too many humans in the past tricked the fey in order to steal their children back."

Hector nodded and added, "Losing to a human is a sign of weakness. It's political death."

"And the other reasons?" Christoffer asked.

"The fey divide into one of four ancient royal political family lines," Aleks said. "These royal houses are Spring, Summer, Autumn, and Winter with special powers attributed to each."

"Yes," Hector agreed. "Spring for renewal; Summer for growth; Autumn for temperance; and Winter for supremacy."

"Cheery," Geirr grumbled.

"A changeling could be a powerful child from one of these royal families stolen away by another house to upset the balance – as part of a coup perhaps… or a changeling could be a child forsaken by its own house, if those in power sought to protect that power and feared the child would grow up to overthrow them," Hector said.

"I would be killed on sight," Aleks explained.

"We have to go around then," Filip said, his expression brooking no argument.

"There is no way around," Hector said regretfully. "There is only over, through, or under Niffleheim. Over is too visible and impossible as we lack wyverns. Through is even more treacherous. We'd be traveling past their cities and palaces."

"So that leaves under," Geirr said. "Are you okay with that Aleks? We'll only go, if you are comfortable with this plan."

"It's safe?" he asked Hector.

Hector sighed. "Nothing about the fey is safe, but less deadly, certainly."

"They sound as horrible as dragons. Why aren't they captured and put into the Under Realm?" Zaria demanded.

"The worst are. Most of the time, the fey backstab each other. Rarely are other parties involved in their political power grabs. If we leave them alone there's generally nothing to worry about. Now we must get going, or we won't reach the entrance to the underground passage today."

"Isn't darkness better coverage?" Geirr asked. "Not that it gets dark this time of year."

"The entrance only exists at dusk. I suspect to lure in weary unsuspecting travelers."

"Oh goody," Geirr said to Aleks. "I guess that's us."

Christoffer clapped Geirr on the back as they started walking. "Just be glad you're along for the trip. You could be stuck in a featureless room at the bottom of a river."

"I hope I don't regret this," Aleks said grimly.

Zaria saw him look over his shoulder at the ocean. The giants seemed so very far away now. Perhaps Oskar had been right to stop them. Zaria looked ahead and felt even under the bright sun that the road ahead was bleak.

***

"We go down there," Hector said, pointing at the bottom of the well.

"You're kidding," Aleks said, looking down into the depths. "I can see water from here."

"Tis a wishing well," Madam Brown said, peering up at the roof overhead and fingering a rusty chain. "Strange for it to be iron."

"It was swapped out with a wish a long time ago," Hector said. "It was done to keep the fey from getting out."

"Fairies don't like iron," Zaria whispered to Filip, who stood shoulder-to-shoulder with her on the opposite side of the well.

Filip rested his hands on the stone wall. "So, now what? How do we get down?"

"Carefully," Madam Brown told him, giving him a look that said (in Zaria's estimate,) *Duh*.

"You still have your rope, right?" Christoffer asked Aleks.

He nodded and dug into his bag, then pulled out a coil and placed it on the ledge. "Check."

Christoffer reached out and plucked it up. He started messing with the ends, and Aleks snatched it back. "Someone should tie it to the beam, not you, obviously, as you apparently don't know knots."

"Me neither," Geirr said, shaking his head.

"Don't you know sailing knots?" Zaria asked Aleks.

Hector didn't say anything as the friends talked. He put down his bag and consulted its contents. He pulled out items one by one and set them on the ground, making a nest inside before replacing them.

"Madam Brown," Hector said, gesturing to his sack. "You'll be safer here as we travel."

She sniffed. "I tis not afraid."

"They'll enslave you if they catch you."

"Tis not a bad life, I still get to do what I do best."

"Indulge me," Hector pleaded. "I don't want to chance it."

She nodded, but frowned. Zaria and Christoffer watched as she shrank in size and climbed into the nest. She looked up at Hector.

"For Hart," she said.

"For Hart," he agreed and closed the bag. He stood and reached into his pockets. He fished something out and held it to Zaria. "Princess."

She took it and realized it was a gold coin. Flipping it over, Zaria admired the raised floral design. "What's this?"

"A token for the well," he said. "Make a wish and toss it in. If your wish is worthy, it will be granted. If it isn't, it won't be, but a wish must be made to reveal the passage."

Zaria pressed her lips together and thought for a moment. She looked at the others and at the coin. She had her wish. Tossing the coin in the air, Zaria prayed and wished for Aleks' safety.

As it descended into the well, Zaria leaned over and saw the specter pluck the coin from the air and sink below the surface with it. She gasped and stumbled back in alarm at the fleshy sighting.

Filip caught her and set her aright. She shook all over. How had it done that? Filip rubbed her arms briskly, trying to erase the sudden appearance of gooseflesh.

"Are you okay?" he asked.

Zaria jerked upright and stepped away from him, running her sweaty palms over her leggings. "Fine," she said, not looking at him.

"Zar-Zar –" Filip started.

"Guys, do you see what I see?" Christoffer interrupted, pointing into the well.

Zaria lunged for the stone wall and peered over. She half-expected to see the trollish specter again, with Christoffer as eye-witness to the thing haunting her. Instead, she saw the water drain away completely, revealing a glittery golden floor full of coins.

Hector took Aleks' halfway knotted rope and tied it efficiently to the overhead beam. He tugged it twice to check its hold and then handed the end to Geirr.

"Start climbing down," Hector ordered.

"Me?" Geirr said, stunned. He looked into the well. "I – uh... do I have to be first?"

"I'll go!" Christoffer volunteered. He took the rope, slung it into the well.

Zaria watched him clamber onto the ledge and swing his legs in. "Be careful," she warned.

"Piece of cake," Christoffer said with a jaunty smile. "It's like rock climbing, only easier."

Then he disappeared over the ledge. Zaria and the others watched his descent. He leaned back, keeping his feet above his head and walked down the wall. In moments he was at the bottom. His feet rustled the coins matting the floor. They made a shimmery curtain of sound as they shifted on the floor.

"Don't touch the coins with your hands," Hector admonished, as Christoffer leaned over to do just that.

Christoffer yanked his hand back and stood up. "Righty-o then. Why?"

"Because they belong to the well now," Hector said, helping Zaria up onto the ledge. "If you steal one, you'll also belong to the well. Permanently."

"I was just going to look!" Christoffer whined.

"Better to be safe than sorry," Hector returned. He looked Zaria over and stared her straight in the eye. "Ready, Princess?" She nodded. "Good, just copy what Christoffer did."

Zaria concentrated on her footwork and lowered herself steadily. She glanced up at the ring of faces watching her. Filip waved. Looking down, she saw Christoffer. It didn't seem too far – and then she slipped, slamming into the side wall. Dangling in the air, it suddenly seemed very far indeed. As she scrabbled for footing, her heart did a crazy, *thump, thump, thump* in her chest.

"ZARIA!" Aleks and Geirr shouted at once.

"Breathe," Christoffer called to her. "Steady, steady. You're halfway there. You got this. Listen to my voice."

Zaria let Christoffer coach her to the floor. Her knees felt wobbly, but she was grateful to be on the ground. Christoffer gave her a hug.

"You next, Geirr," he called up.

"Great," Geirr said, scrambling up and over the edge of the well. "You fly planes; you're not afraid of heights," he told himself, before lowering himself down.

The whole way he kept a death-grip on the rope. In a few moments, Geirr made it to the floor of the well, landing with a loud *clink-clink-clink*. He was followed by Filip, who managed it with a breezy ease of honed athleticism. Aleks, also a rock climber, had no trouble on the way down. Hector joined them last, and when his feet touched the ground, the rope disappeared.

"That's not a good sign," Aleks observed darkly.

Hector gripped his shoulder and released it, walking away. "This way everyone – the passage is over here."

A small opening, blocked with golden coins, waited for them. Hector got down on his hands and knees and scooped armfuls of coins back to the center of the well. When room was made, he crawled through the opening. Coins cascaded after him.

The children followed, Aleks coming through last, shot another worried glance up at the opening of the well. Zaria and Geirr helped him through and they stood in a narrow stone passageway.

"Check your sleeves, socks, and shoes," Hector said, turning on a flashlight. "You don't want to take any coins with you."

The friends did that quickly. Aleks checked thrice and nodded to the others when he was ready. Filip handed out flashlights to everyone. Zaria clicked hers on as Aleks sneaked his hand into her own and squeezed.

She looked over at him, but he wouldn't look at her. She squared her shoulders, aimed her flashlight ahead and squeezed his hand back.

Chapter Seven: Crossing the Plains of Niffleheim

The underground passageway opened into a large obsidian cavern. It was so vast that Zaria couldn't see the edges of it; even their flashlights weren't much use as they didn't shine very far into the impenetrable darkness surrounding them. The cavern was cold too. Her breath fogged in front of her with every exhalation. As she waved her flashlight about her she saw that the ceiling was covered in smooth icy formations, like scallops or Norwick's scales.

Aleks still held her hand, but his hold was slack. His initial terror retreated as they traveled without encountering anyone or anything. He was silent, although that could be because Christoffer was peppering Hector with questions about the fey.

"We'll camp here for the night," Hector said, indicating the left side of the tunnel they'd emerged from.

"Oh good," Geirr said. "I'm beat." He slung his backpack on the ground and pulled out his water bottle to drink.

"We'll cross the plains tomorrow and hopefully be back topside by nightfall. There is much to do in the meantime."

Aleks let go of Zaria's hand to unhitch the tent he'd carried. Christoffer did the same with his tent, pulling it out of its carrying sleeve. Zaria and Filip helped to raise them, laughing as they messed up and one of the tents collapsed.

Hector released Madam Brown, and together they went off to find something to eat and drink. They traveled so far that Zaria couldn't see Hector's flashlight anymore. That made her nervous, but she didn't say anything for fear of drawing the Stag Lord's absence to Aleks' notice.

"This has been an awesome adventure," Christoffer said with a happy sigh, shucking off his shoes and crawling inside his tent.

Zaria peeked inside to watch Christoffer arrange his sleeping bag. She handed him hers. "Everything you'd hoped it would be?" she asked wryly.

He nodded vigorously. "Trolls, pirate adventures, humpback whales, giants, wishing wells, cursed golden coins, and spelunking through fey territory – what's not to love?"

"Well to be fair, mate," Filip said, peeking through the tent from the other side. "The pirate adventures weren't really piratey at all."

"Don't care," Christoffer singsonged. "It counts."

"Sure, it does," Geirr said from nearby. He was inside Aleks' tent. "It counts about as much as Filip being a knight."

"I could, too, be a knight," Filip called back, leaving Christoffer's tent to argue his knightly merits with Geirr.

Zaria shook her head and crawled inside the tent. She sat Indian-style on her sleeping bag and hugged her small travel pillow. Christoffer found a pack of raisins and opened it. He offered her some, but Zaria declined. She did not like raisins. Grapes, yes; raisins, no.

"You don't seem like you're having fun," Christoffer said, poking at his raisins.

"I'm worried," Zaria said defensively. "You're treating this whole thing like it's a lark."

"Weren't you excited by everything when you first forayed into the magical side of Norway?" he countered.

Zaria shrugged. She picked at the tag attached to the pillow, twisting it between her fingers. "That was before I traded Hart to Olaf."

Christoffer tossed a raisin in the air and tried to catch it. When he missed, he tried again and grinned when it landed perfectly in his mouth. "You're too hard on yourself. Aren't we on an adventure to fix that now?"

"I suppose," she mumbled, hugging the pillow tighter. "I keep waiting for the other shoe to drop."

Christoffer touched her shoulder. "Why? What do we have that Olaf wants now?"

"We're going to have the sword," she reminded him.

Christoffer tossed another raisin. "But we're going to use it to free Hart, not to exchange for Hart."

"It's not just Hart," Zaria said after a minute. She wanted him to understand. "I'm not able to sleep."

"Want to tell me about it?" he asked, digging out the last of the raisins and popping them into his mouth.

A loud ripping sound startled them as a claw rent the fabric of the tent in two. Zaria shrieked as a red fox's head poked inside. Christoffer grabbed her by the arm and hauled her back. They cowered against the far side of the tent as another fox's head poked inside just above the first, followed by a third.

"Why, look at what we have here," the first one said. "Humans."

"We haven't had human trespassers in a long time."

"We'll have fun with you morsels."

Christoffer tugged her shoulder again, when Filip and Geirr pushed through the entrance of the tent. They had heard her shriek. Zaria grabbed Filip's outstretched hand and scrambled out of the tent.

The foxes pulled their heads out of the tent and faced the children. A shimmer of multicolored lights engulfed the foxes, and then, standing in their place, were tall, lithe humanoids with sharp faces, huge glittering eyes, red hair, freckles, and pointed ears.

They were fey!

Zaria glanced around wildly for Aleks. He trembled at the back of the group, nearly hidden by Geirr and Filip, but not hidden enough. She spun back around and planted herself at the front. Where were Hector and Madam Brown?

"We are not trespassing," Zaria said, glowering at them.

"Oh ho," the shortest of the three fey said. "Did you hear that, Lukas, not trespassing! How did you get down here?"

"I made a wish," Zaria replied.

The tallest fairy, Lukas, scoffed. "With what coin?" He brushed feathery bangs from his forehead and crossed his arms. "The wishing well only uses our currency. Where did you come by it, except for stealing it in the first place from our vaults?"

"How did you find us?" Filip demanded, stepping beside Zaria.

"Could smell you, we could," said the middle fairy. "You can't sneak by us. You stink."

Were they really smelling them or were they smelling Aleks? The mountain-troll king of Trolgar sniffed out Aleks' changeling status at first meeting last year. Zaria chanced a look behind her at Aleks. Geirr stood in front of him and Christoffer too. Aleks was looking down at his shoes, trying not to draw the fairies' attention.

"What do you want?" Zaria demanded.

"What do we want, Isak?" the shortest fairy asked the middle one.

"All trespassers become permanent members of our courts," Isak said. "My uncle will be most pleased with your addition. We can always use more runts."

"Runts?" Geirr asked, crossing his arms and planting his feet.

Lukas grinned, his dark brown eyes bright with mischief. "Runts are slaves. Aski, round them up."

The shortest cracked his knuckles and waved his hands. Zaria felt something wrap around her legs. She looked down and gasped. Climbing up her legs were tree roots. Christoffer and Geirr shouted in alarm as they noticed too. Filip grunted. Zaria gripped one and yanked hard. It crumbled, but others grew to replace it, too thick to break.

Aski laughed. "Now, now," he said, shaking a finger at her. "No struggling. The roots won't like it, and you won't like the consequences."

"You have no right!" Zaria spat, struggling against her bindings.

"You're in the lands of the Autumn Court, uninvited. We have every right," Lukas said dismissively, waving a regal hand. "Isak, watch the girl; she's going to be a handful. We must return and report as soon as possible. We can send someone for their things later."

As the fey departed, the roots began to drag Zaria and the boys forward. Zaria tried to dig her feet into the ground to halt her momentum, but the pull was irresistible. They were dragged into the darkness.

The inky blackness wasn't any trouble for the fey, as they transformed back into foxes. Zaria was sure they had innate night vision, which was vastly unfair. Zaria tripped every few steps over the uneven floor, nearly falling to the ground several times in her fight against the roots. She could hear the others faltering alongside her too. Each grunt and groan both reassured her and worried her.

It wasn't long before she went sprawling, landing face-first into the dirt. Two of the boys tripped over her and landed in a heap beside her. She heard Geirr groan from her right.

"Zaria," Filip grunted. "Are you okay? I didn't mean to kick you."

"Fine," she hissed, as the roots yanked her into a sitting position. "I hate these things!"

"Me too," Geirr huffed. "Each one I break grows back thicker and stronger."

Christoffer scoffed. "You think that's bad? I'm going to have bruises on my bruises."

"How about you Aleks?" Zaria asked. "Are you all right?"

Her question was met by silence.

"Aleks?" Geirr repeated. "Come on mate, speak up."

"If you can't talk at least grunt," Filip muttered, groaning a second later as he collided with Zaria again, toppling them over in a tangle of limbs and bony elbows.

"Aleks?" Christoffer tried again.

"Where is he?" Zaria whispered. She put her hands in front of her face and waved them around.

"Watch it," Filip complained when she accidentally smacked him.

"Almost got it," Christoffer grunted.

"Got what?" said Geirr.

A beam of light lit the darkness and revealed that Aleks wasn't with them at all. Christoffer's light shone all around, bouncing off the cavern walls and ceiling. Aleks wasn't anywhere near them. Then unblinking eyes appeared, glowing starkly in the light.

The foxes reemerged, and Isak transformed into his handsome self, with chiseled jaw and sharp nose.

"Don't dally, runts," he said. "You don't want to make us angry."

"Here's a problem, nimrod," Zaria said, raising her nose up. "We can't see in the dark."

Isak stared at her unblinking. "You have light now," he said, gesturing to the flashlight. "Get moving."

He turned and melted into his fox form and slipped off. Zaria slumped and was dragged by the roots again even more insistently than before. She stumbled, tripped, and lurched forward, her awkwardness copied by the others as they, too, were forced to follow.

Geirr attempted still to break free, but the more he fought, the higher the roots climbed until they had his arms encased and trapped at his sides. He was forced to hop and the indignity of it made his skin flush darkly.

Somewhere along the way they had climbed upward, the path so gradual Zaria hadn't noticed. The darkness was no longer absolute. Light from somewhere faintly lit the space. It was the type of dim light that made one squint to see more but revealed less. Then the shadowed form of the foxes appeared and soon after, Zaria could make out the colors of their red pelts.

Light blinded the quartet as they rounded a bend in the cavern. The foxes slipped through a small opening at the base of the floor. Their tails whipping out of sight, as they dashed ahead of the children.

"Do we get on hands and knees and crawl through or let these magical roots yank us through?" Geirr groused, trying to hop backward with little effect.

For Zaria there was little choice in the matter, she reached the opening first and was banged into the wall like a rag doll. She forced her hands out through the confining body wrap and braced against the wall.

Filip and Christoffer reached her next. Each one tossed at the wall at odd angles. Filip banged his shoulder and slid down into an ignominious heap.

"Ow," he muttered dryly, just before the roots began to ripple violently.

The roots moved like crawling bugs over his body. They backed Filip away from the wall and flattened him out onto his back. He shaded his eyes as the sunlight hit him directly in the face.

"Filip grab the opening!" Zaria cried out in warning, but it was too late.

Within moments the roots had carried him on his back through the hole and out of sight.

"That settles that question," Geirr grumbled, hopping twice toward the wall. "We crawl through – wouldn't do to let him go by himself."

"Sure wouldn't," Christoffer agreed as he got to his hands and knees and crawled toward the opening, becoming a black shadow in the bright light. "I think it'll be okay, my bonds are loosening. Just keep a clear head."

"Comforting. The roots strangle us the rest of the time, but if we willingly go in the direction of our captors then they loosen. I'm comforted, aren't you?" Geirr asked Zaria.

"No, but Christoffer's right, you know. We can't let him go alone."

Zaria's quivering arms collapsed. She had just enough time to push herself far from the stone wall so as not to bang her head. She twisted to land on her hands and knees. Taking Christoffer's lead, she crawled forward and found her restraints easing, making the passage easy.

She looked behind her and saw Geirr copying her. His roots loosened to give him range of movement. He wasn't happy about following them into the fairies' trap, but he followed. And that counted for a lot, thought Zaria.

The low tunnel grew larger after a short distance. When she could stand, she did. Wherever they were, the sunlight pooled over everything, appearing to drape over all like a thick curtain. Despite the sunshine, the air still smelled slightly stale, as if they hadn't left the underground.

Zaria blinked rapidly trying to clear the sunspots dancing across her vision. Once she could see, she saw rainbows. Thousands of them refracted and reflected everywhere. They bounced from every surface, and every surface redoubled them, as if the surfaces were made of glass or ice.

"It's like a unicorn projectile-vomited all over everything," Geirr complained, squinting.

Christoffer laughed. "It comes from up there," he said, pointing to the low ceilings. "The ice scallop ceiling acts like a prism."

It was beautiful and similar in some aspects to Álfheim, the elves' home, with its delicate frosted glass structures. Both cities twinkled, sparkled, and shone even in the dullest light. That, however, was where the similarities ended.

The fey's structures were blockier, solid, and heavy. It was the difference between the decorative and fanciful elements of Rococo design and Soviet era concrete block architecture. There was a harshness in the fey's construction that was absent within the elves' engineering.

Every building looked the same and was precisely situated under the ceiling to ensure the best use of light in the underground space. Each surface was cut at exact angles and worn smooth and flat. No irregularities or imperfections would disturb the material's ability to catch sunlight and throw rainbows. It was meticulous and uniform; grand at once for its austerity and reflected radiance.

Zaria noticed then that her bindings were gone. Exclaiming, she pointed to Christoffer and Geirr. Theirs were also gone. She looked around for Filip and found him wandering an empty circular space at the center of the city. She raced over to him.

"You gave us a fright," she told him.

"This place is something, isn't it?" he said abstractedly, running a hand over a wall.

"Where are the foxes?" she asked, looking around nervously.

Out of the corner of her eye, something flickered. Then she saw it. A shriek lodged in her throat as her hideous specter whispered in and out of the building's surfaces. And then it did something it had never done before – it stepped out of its reflective surface and took form – materializing before her in all its ugliness, leering at her.

Then she did scream.

Chapter Eight: Prism Break

Her screams brought everyone running. Friends and foes appeared, but Zaria didn't care. She shook from head-to-toe like a leaf.

"Did you see it?" she cried desperately. She grabbed Filip's shirt and shook him. "Did you see it?"

He shook his head, blond hair falling into his face, and she let him go. Spinning around she tried to find it and spotted the thing behind the crowd. The creature wore her clothes, copied her hair style, and stared back at her with yellow eyes, streaked with purple. The only thing different was its golden footwear. It winked and slipped back into the prismatic surface of an imposing building.

She pointed at it. "There, it was right there!"

A few in the crowd looked over their shoulders to where she pointed. There was nothing to see. The trollish specter was gone. Filip touched her arm and shook his head again. Zaria slumped in defeat. She wiped her nose and rubbed her eyes. Clearly the lack of good sleep was getting to her.

"This one is a raving lunatic, Lukas," a cold female said, turning back to face them.

Zaria stared mutinously at the woman until the fairy raised one supercilious brow in derision. She sniffed and stared down her pointy nose in a superior manner.

The female said frostily, "She'll come to nothing good."

"Now, now, Nori," Lukas taunted softly from her right. "She might be handier to have around than we know. The girl said she wished on the Lost Well."

"Did she?" Nori sniffed again, which irritated Zaria. She wanted to tell the gorgeous fairy to blow her nose.

"These humans will serve our father well. I am certain of it. Besides it has been many years since any son of man was so foolish as to cross into our realm."

Nori shook back a waterfall of red curls. "Very well," she said haughtily. "By all means present the runts to Grimkell. It'll be your funeral."

"Jealous, sister?" Lukas asked, delighted with Nori's petulance.

As Zaria predicted, Nori sniffed. The fairy inspected her cuticles and said, "Of course not."

The condescension in those words was so thick one could choke on it. Nori probably hoped her brother would. Lukas chucked Nori under her chin and gave her a biting smile.

"Or perhaps," he said, softly sneering. "They will be just the edge I need to eclipse you in Grimkell's favor."

"You could bring him a hundred children of man, and he still would prefer me to you."

"So confident are you? How many times have you failed him recently?"

Nori's face sharpened in distaste. "Take your runts and get out of my hair."

"Runts," Lukas said insouciantly, waving an imperious hand. "Follow, and do keep together. Wandering off will lead to certain death and other unpleasantness."

Zaria gulped and stuffed her hands under her arms. She felt small. She glanced anxiously at the passing buildings, looking for her tormentor. The only comfort in all of this was her friends. They bracketed her on either side, offering her protection. Filip tried to catch her eye, but she looked away, glancing down at her shoes, uncertain and confused.

***

Zaria wasn't happy about entering the grand building into which the specter had disappeared, having made its daring escape. She would have rather gone into any other building. She kept glancing into their reflections as they were escorted through the opulent corridors looking for the ghostly thing. Even though she never saw it, her gut still tightened with worry. When would it visit her next?

All around them, the walls were opalescent and glossy, polished to perfection. The tinted glass acted like mirrors throwing their reflection out into infinity, until like a fun house, Zaria didn't know where reality began and fantasy ended. She missed Aleks in that moment, because she knew he would have known how to navigate the halls.

As Zaria looked around, she wondered if the treated glass permitted privacy or spying. She touched a wall, feeling the cold blemish-free surface. It was slick and smooth, just like it looked. If a wall could be given to feelings, she would describe it as aloof, just like its inhabitants.

After several more twists and turns, Lukas, Isak, and Aski stopped them outside a door without a doorknob that blended nearly seamlessly into the hallway. Lukas tapped the top right corner and the door clicked sharply like the sound of a finger-snap and slid back. He stepped through unannounced, but before Filip and Geirr could follow, Isak halted them.

"We wait," he said ominously.

Zaria shifted nervously from foot to foot until Christoffer laid a calming hand on her shoulder. Her nervous energy didn't evaporate under the gentle pressure, so she fiddled with her zipper-pull.

Christoffer, on the other hand, was relaxed. He stretched and yawned and slumped against the wall. Aski glared at him, but Christoffer ignored the fairy.

Lukas returned and summoned the others. Aski pushed Christoffer off the wall and herded them through the opening. Isak and Lukas strode ahead.

"Welcome to the Great Fox Hall," Lukas called delightedly over his shoulder. He waved a hand to indicate the room at large.

And it was large. The space was as elegant as it was cavernous. Its true dimensions were warped like the corridor. Long slate tables with benches were lined up in two rows on either side. The prismatic walls made it look more like eighty rows. Huge floor candelabras stood sentinel between every table with smaller candelabras sitting midway on the tables.

At the far end of the room on a raised platform sat a regal figure playing a table board game alone. His graying red hair was long and neatly tied at the nape of his neck. It was hard to see with his massive fur collar. This must be Grimkell. His hook nose and keen eyes tracked them as they moved through the space.

Lukas clicked his heels together and bowed. "The runts, Father."

"Good, good. Have the girl come forward," Grimkell said absently, concentrating on the board.

Isak guided Zaria by the arm to Lukas, who then propelled her up the stage.

Grimkell waved to the seat opposite him. "Sit."

Zaria ignored him and studied the board. It was circular with small holes punctuating the entire surface. In some of the holes, tall slender pegs made from a reddish wood rested. The pegs were modestly carved and vaguely resembled foxes.

"Do you play?" he asked.

"What is the game? Chinese Checkers?"

Grimkell flashed a smile which was more teeth than friendliness. "No. It's a game invented by our ancestors, and was once played by Vikings, until the humans forgot it."

Zaria glared. "Then why did you ask if I could play it?"

"Because you found the Lost Well. The fey haven't seen it since the time of the Vikings, when we aided Queen Helena in creating the Under Realm. It was unlikely, but still possible, for you to know of kettupeli."

"You helped Queen Helena build the void to imprison the world's dragons?"

Grimkell nodded, grabbing pegs from the side of the game and placing them back into the board. "In exchange we were to be left alone to our own pursuits. Had we known the well would vanish, we would not have agreed."

Zaria tilted her head. "What's so special about the well?"

Grimkell looked past her to Lukas. "If the boys are like her, then their usefulness is not something I would count on."

Lukas sighed with disgust. "I do apologize, Father. I expected her to know something useful."

Zaria gave the pretty fey her best stink eye. "I am not dumb. I just don't know why the Lost Well is important to you."

"Your intelligence remains to be seen. As for the Lost Well, whichever fey court controls it is automatically the ruler of the other three. There is much power in the well. Now, we'll play the first version of kettupeli. Sit," Grimkell ordered.

Zaria sat. Grimkell nodded with satisfaction and proceeded to explain the first variant of the game. His long elegant fingers plucked a peg from the board. There were fifty-one pegs and fifty-two holes. They would draw an equal number of pegs, with the extra peg forfeited at the end.

He showed her the underside, explaining that each peg was colored at its base. In the game there were thirty black, ten red, five blue, three green, two yellow, and one white peg. Each color was worth a specific number of points based on the odds of drawing the color, with white being worth the most at one hundred points.

"We take turns, drawing one peg at a time. At the end we tally up the points and the winner is the one with the most."

"That sounds easy enough."

"Why don't you draw first," Grimkell offered. "I shall reset the board." He spun it around twice and then waved at her to go ahead.

"That's it?" she asked.

Grimkell nodded. "Magic is useful."

Zaria agreed. She reached out and took one from the middle of the board. She drew a black, one point. Grimkell also chose from the middle. Black. They were tied. Several turns passed this way as they each drew a black peg.

Things got interesting when Zaria drew the first non-black color. It was green and worth twenty points. That put her in the lead. Grimkell pulled a red worth two points. Zaria drew another black. Grimkell another red.

The board was emptying fast and the odds for colors were getting higher. Zaria chose again and got another green. Only one left in the game, which made her feel great until Grimkell drew a yellow. That peg caught him up, giving him fifty points, and now he surpassed her.

She drew a blue, closing the gap in their scores by ten points. He drew another red. She a black. Soon they were down to the last turn with three pegs left. Zaria had one hundred twenty-three points; Grimkell one hundred six. It was anyone's game. There was a black, a blue, and the white peg remaining. Zaria would win as long as Grimkell didn't pick the white peg.

Zaria drew the blue peg. Grimkell's odds were fifty-fifty. She watched raptly as his long fingers hesitated over a peg and then pulled it. It was black. Zaria won. She danced in her seat with excitement.

"Now let's talk about the Lost Well," Grimkell said, gathering the pegs and setting them back in the board. "You will take me to it."

Zaria narrowed her eyes at him. "Why should I? What's in it for me?"

"Yeah," echoed Christoffer. "What's in it for us?"

Lukas rolled his eyes and made a motion to Isak and Aski. Christoffer was hauled out of the chamber kicking and shouting. Filip and Geirr looked back and forth between Christoffer and Zaria.

"Where are you taking Christoffer?" Geirr asked.

"Just to the hallway where he cannot disturb the talks," Lukas replied. "Now, do be quiet."

Grimkell analyzed Zaria the way he had the kettupeli board. Eventually he sat back, and with a too-pleased expression, he offered a deal with the devil.

"Zaria, was it? I propose a game; the winner gets one favor from the other. Surely there is something you want from me…" he trailed off leaving a suggestive silence.

Zaria stared at her hands, then out to her friends, and thought about Aleks. Maybe, if she worded her favor right, she could protect him… Madam Brown and Hector, too. She nodded and taking a deep breath to calm her nerves, said, "I want safe passage for me and my friends into Jerndor."

"Into Jerndor?" Grimkell asked, diverted. "My, my, my, you are something. What do you wish to do with dwarves?"

"Does it matter?" Zaria challenged.

Grimkell shook his head. "Not at all. Done. If you win, I will personally see to your safe passage. If I win then you will take me to the Lost Well."

"It shouldn't be one game," Zaria inserted quickly. "It should be best two of three."

Grimkell shrugged. "The fey like sport, Princess. Whether I win once or twice doesn't matter. Let us make this more interesting. Champions can be picked to play rather than you or me competing personally."

"It should be fair, too," Zaria added. "No personal magic. No cheating. All challenges agreed to before we start; including order of play."

Grimkell laughed again. "I think I like you, girl. Lukas, you did well after all."

"Thank you, Father."

"Let the games begin," Grimkell said gleefully.

Chapter Nine: Testing Mettle, Grit, and Wits

"There should be a test of strength, a test of endurance, and a test of intelligence," Lukas offered, as Grimkell and Zaria stepped away from the platform and joined the others.

Isak and Aski re-entered the room with Christoffer. Zaria watched her friend rub his wrists and shake his shoulders.

"Are you all right?" Filip asked him.

"Yeah," Christoffer said. "No thanks to these fox-heads."

"Zaria has just made a deal with Grimkell," Geirr informed him.

"Oh? What is it?" Christoffer asked.

Zaria smiled brightly. "Grimkell will provide safe passage into Jerndor for all of my friends, if we win two of three challenges."

She was thinking of Aleks and Hector and Madam Brown. She watched Christoffer's eyes widen, as he realized that too. His nod of approval gave her a warm fuzzy feeling. She liked having the upper hand in negotiations.

"And if you lose, Zaria will guide me to the Lost Well, where I will recover the magic there for my people," Grimkell said. Then he smiled. "And of course, you will all be stuck in our prismatic void forever."

"As our slaves," Lukas added, to remind them.

Zaria frowned. "That wasn't stated."

"It was implied," Lukas said with a smirk. "After all, you're already runts. Grimkell is being magnanimous in granting you a chance to win your freedom. Most runts aren't so lucky. You should be grateful."

"Oh we are," Geirr said sarcastically. "Ever so much."

"What are these challenges?" asked Christoffer.

Grimkell gave Lukas an affectionate slap on the back. "My son has suggested three types of challenges. Endurance, strength, and intelligence. The fey are proud to be the best at all three, and I think it fair. Don't you, girl?"

Zaria nodded. "Yes," she agreed slowly. "What shall be the endurance test?"

"Swimming," Isak said. "Perhaps a race across the inland sea?"

"That measures speed, not endurance," said Christoffer, rejecting the challenge. "How about holding one's breath? Three challengers for each team can compete. The winner will be the team with the most time spent underwater."

"The time is added up and shared collectively," Grimkell rubbed his chin and nodded. "I like it. Accepted. Now for strength."

"Wrestling?" Aski offered. "I love wrestling. Win condition could be the surrender of the other competitor or their death." He cracked his knuckles and twitched his shoulders.

Filip shook his head. "While Geirr and I wrestle at school, you have several stones on us. We wouldn't be evenly matched."

"A game of tug-o-war then," Aski replied with a shrug. "It makes no difference to me."

"Three people on each team?" Zaria offered.

She pictured something like American physical education classes with a long rope, a piece of cloth marking the middle, and a line in the dirt. She didn't relish the idea of rope burns on her hands.

Grimkell dismissed that idea with a wave. "Better challenge is one on one, like Viking tradition."

"What's that?" Christoffer asked.

"Aski, Isak, please demonstrate," Grimkell said.

They did as requested and quickly sank to the floor. They pressed their feet against each other and Lukas provided his handkerchief which Aski knotted quickly into a basic loop. The two fey pulled, leaning back and straightening their legs, until Isak relaxed and was quickly pulled forward and thrown over Aski's head.

"That's how we play tug-o-war," Grimkell explained. "The first one to be tossed loses."

Aski helped Isak up and the two grinned. Isak twitched his shoulders, relaxing his stance. He said, "It's better than arm wrestling. It requires full body strength, not just a single strong limb."

"And of course, for intelligence we should play a round of kettupeli."

"The first version," Zaria said.

"The first version is more chance than strategy," Grimkell said. He clapped his hands. "No, we play the second version. I will give you a practice round, before we play for real. Fair?"

Zaria looked to the others. Filip shrugged. "Seems fair enough."

Zaria nodded. "Okay then. We have the challenges. I think the order of play should be kettupeli, breath-holding, and tug-o-war."

Grimkell nodded. "I have no problem with that. Let's head back to the board."

As they retook their positions at the head table, Grimkell began to explain the second version of kettupeli. The goal was to draw the pegs in succession of the most probable color to the least probable color (black, red, blue, green, yellow, and white). If a player made a mistake, the player's turn ended and all the pegs were returned to the board.

They played a round for practice. Nothing much happened. They both drew double black and returned the pegs to the board. That was all the practice Zaria was going to get before the game began.

"Magic in the pegs blanks out the colors as they are returned to the board so the opposing player can't cheat. Would you care to go first or second, Princess?"

Zaria gave him a startled look.

Grimkell's vulpine smile gave Zaria shivers. "You look like your mother," he said conversationally. "You share the same glowing skin color, gleaming dark hair, and purple eyes. One must wonder why she let you sneak into the fairy realm. Perhaps Queen Helena wishes to trade with Niffleheim once more?"

"You go first," Zaria said to him, ignoring his probing.

Grimkell spun the board. "To refresh the pegs," he said, reminding her that the game resets with a spin. "Now we are ready to begin."

He plucked a peg and revealed its underside. Black. He placed it on the table and plucked another peg. Also black. Scooping up both pegs, Grimkell replaced them on the board. As Zaria watched, she saw the colors disappear from the pegs as Grimkell brought them close to the board. When he was done, he waved a hand to indicate for her to go.

Zaria pulled one at random. Black. She pulled another. Black. She replaced them, putting one of her pegs into the originally empty fifty-second hole. It didn't make sense to leave the obvious open space in the center of the board untouched.

Play proceeded. Grimkell drew another two blacks. Zaria a blue. Grimkell drew a black and a green. Zaria watched keenly to see where he placed his pegs. A red still needed to be found. The more she played, the easier the game seemed, even though it was frustrating to watch black after black appear. Grimkell then drew a black, a red, her blue, and his green. But he drew another red and had to replace his pegs.

On Zaria's next turn she grabbed one of her blacks, and hesitated. Did she risk pulling from the pegs he replaced or did she try for a red of her own. He'd had two red in five pegs. The odds were higher if she drew from what he replaced than finding a red on the board. She risked it and plucked one of his five. It was red. She wiggled in her chair in delight.

Grimkell stayed silent, fingering the fur collar around his neck, and watched the play with a steely, poker face. Zaria chanced another pick from Grimkell's placement and drew another. She got a yellow. Zaria looked at the peg, startled. How did she get a yellow? She looked at the board again and sighed. She'd probably been off by a peg.

"You can do it, Zar-Zar," Filip encouraged.

She looked over her shoulder and smiled at the boys. She turned back, shuffled her pegs and placed them on the board, careful to put the yellow back where she'd found it in the first place. The black she put in the shifting blank space on the board and the red where the black had been.

Grimkell ignored her pegs entirely on his next turn. He grabbed a black at random it seemed, chose the other red from his original grouping, then blue, then green. Now he hesitated. He stared at her and then the board and decided on one of her pegs. Zaria gripped her seat, praying he wouldn't pick the yellow. Grimkell picked the yellow.

She gave a gusty sigh and folded her arms over the table and rested her head in them. Would he miraculously pull the white or would she get another chance to go?

She waited, watching Grimkell study the board. She knew he was calculating odds and percentages. They must have drawn more than half the pegs available, the white not yet revealed.

Grimkell's shoulders relaxed and he twirled his hand over the board. Then with a flourish he plucked the white peg and revealed it with a triumphant smile.

"How did you do that?" Zaria demanded.

She wondered if the spin of the board really had reset the pegs or not. She couldn't be sure. The other magic Grimkell had described was real, but she thought he found the white peg too easily.

"I've played this game for years, Princess. I know its odds better than anyone. I win. Now for the swimming challenge."

"Breath-holding," Zaria corrected, still upset that she lost.

On one hand she congratulated herself for demanding best two of three, but on the other hand she was very upset to be one loss away from losing the whole thing.

"My apologies. Yes, breath-holding. By all means let us make our way to the inland sea," Grimkell said, his expression slick and his eyes cool.

Zaria could tell he was already counting on his victory. She would not, could not, let the fey win the next challenge. Unfortunately, Zaria didn't know if it would be in her power to stop them from claiming victory. A glance at Christoffer and she could tell he felt the same way. They shared a look and fell in line with their friends as the fey departed from the Great Fox Hall.

***

A large group of fairies followed the small gathering to the inland sea. Almost everyone was in their fey form, but several came as foxes. Gray, red, red sesame, blond and white coats streaked around the edges and through the ankles of the crowd. Everyone vied for a spot to view the competition.

Along the edge of the inland sea, Zaria could make out the blurry shapes of three cityscapes. The diffused light would occasionally glint off a roof. The effect was like a slumberous giant winking. Zaria wondered at their inhabitants.

"Who do you pick Princess, to make up your team of three?" Grimkell asked from the bank, breaking into her musings.

"We can do it," Geirr promised, when she looked at her friends. "You stay and watch. Make sure there's no funny business."

"How long can a fox hold its breath?" Christoffer asked Zaria.

She shrugged. "How do I know?"

Filip nudged them both. "Remember, no personal magic is allowed. Turning into a fox would be use of personal magic."

"Oh, well, that's a relief, I guess," Christoffer said.

"How long can the fey hold their breath?" Geirr asked, watching the murmuring crowd.

"We're about to find out," Zaria said. "I choose my friends to be my champions."

"And I choose my son, my daughter, and my nephew."

Lukas, Nori, and Isak, began disrobing. Their underclothes acted like swimwear. Nori was the first to enter the water, gliding out to the middle in smooth, strong strokes. Lukas followed, giving Zaria a roguish wink before diving in. Zaria fought back a blush. The fey were built like swimmers with strong, lean, long muscles.

The boys were a little more hesitant getting into the sea. Geirr waded in, and gasped. "Norwick's teeth! It's colder than –"

"Don't be a baby," Nori taunted, splashing him with water.

Geirr quit complaining and gulped, eyeing the beautiful fey creature as one would a predator. She swam in lazy circles around Geirr. He tried to track her, but flopped in the water like a drowning fish.

Christoffer edged closer to the water, a look of supreme concentration on his face as waves lapped over his toes. He gritted his teeth and staunchly strode forward, sinking quickly up to his waist.

"Come on Filip, get in here," he called back before sinking under the water to get his hair wet.

"I guess that's my cue," Filip said.

Zaria touched his elbow. "You can do this," she said.

Filip nodded, took a few steps backward and ran full tilt toward the water. He jumped and cannonballed into the sea. Nori shrieked and lurched backwards. Zaria laughed delightedly, happy to see the female fey discomposed.

Grimkell stepped closer to her and raised his hands. The fey in the water ceased splashing. Lukas dipped down until his nose skimmed the surface. His gleaming eyes tracked his father's every move.

"The team with the longest time under the water wins this challenge. Once you break the water's surface, you are out of the competition, even if you don't draw breath."

"Remember the rules," Zaria added. "No personal magic."

Grimkell's eyes gleamed. "You heard her. Now on the count of three... one, two, three!"

The fey slipped quietly beneath the surface. All three boys took big gulps of air and dunked. The fey on the sidelines tittered in amusement. Zaria watched the crowd, gazed at the distant cities, and refocused on the water's surface. She held her breath with them, counting the seconds as they ticked by.

The water grew agitated. White foam frothed and fizzed along its surface. Zaria tried to make out the shapes beneath, but they were dark and blurred.

"What's going on?" she demanded.

"The drowning of your friends, I believe," Grimkell said throwing her a wicked smile.

"That's cheating!"

"Is it?" Grimkell asked mildly. "I don't think so. Your friends are free to come up for air."

"Unfair sportsmanship is what it is, Lord Grimkell, and it is beneath you," an angry voice boomed from behind.

Chapter Ten: The
Last Challenge

Zaria spun around. "Hector!"

She relaxed at the sight of him, feeling instantly safer with the Stag Lord back. Hector's glowering form parted the fey crowd easily. He tossed his bag down on the ground and got into Grimkell's face, almost poking the fairy's eye out with an antler. Grimkell didn't budge.

"Can't win against human children without being dishonorable?"

"And that from the Prince of Chicanery himself," Grimkell laughed. "Pot meet kettle. Your great-grandfather's duplicity is at the heart of this all. Your kind and Queen Helena played us false."

Hector used his large size to intimidate. "Drowning those children will result in your forfeit," he growled.

Grimkell raised a brow. "Will it? I don't see it that way, especially since we don't plan to kill them."

"But it isn't fair!" Zaria hissed. "We agreed that these challenges must be played fair."

Grimkell raised his palm silencing her. "Your friends are as capable at drowning their competition as my family is at drowning theirs. This is an endurance challenge, based on the ability to hold one's breath; not a friendly stroll in the park."

Christoffer broke the surface first, gasping and choking. He spat out water and shouted, "You lying no-good, cheating, foxfaces!"

Nori broke the surface next. She sputtered and spat out a mouthful of water. When she saw she was second out, she smacked the water in frustration and waded to shore. She climbed to her feet.

"I'm sorry, Father. I meant to stay under longer, but this one –" she pointed a long finger accusingly at Christoffer, "– kicked me in the chest."

"And I'd do it again, you underhanded –"

"Enough, Christoffer," Hector intoned warningly. He stared at Grimkell, and asked, "What were the terms?"

"Fair play, no cheating, and no personal magic," Zaria rattled off, crossing her arms.

She couldn't tear her eyes from the water's surface. Christoffer dripped sulkily beside her, staring at churning water. Her heart was in her throat as she worried about Geirr and Filip.

"And the stakes?" Hector prodded.

"The location of the Lost Well or our freedom and safe passage into Jerndor," Zaria said.

Hector relaxed. "How many challenges?"

"Best two of three. We lost one already," Christoffer said.

Hector folded his arms and turned to watch the water. His expression, though intent, was calm. Zaria sidled closer, wishing for some of his levelheadedness.

"I think we're going to lose," she confided softly. "How much longer can they hold out?"

"As long as we need them too," Hector replied. He nudged her gently. "It'll be okay, Princess."

"How?" she asked miserably.

The water's surface broke again and Isak appeared. A seething Filip followed shortly after. He took in great gulps of air, wheezing like a suffocating fish. The two competitors strode to the shore. A flicker of movement danced along the peripheral of Zaria's vision, but when she looked up she simply saw

Christoffer as he gathered Filip and slapped him on the back a few times, helping to get the water out of Filip's lungs.

The surface of the water calmed, and as it calmed it turned red with blood. Zaria craned her neck trying to see what was happening. She couldn't make anything out. Was Geirr okay? Where was Lukas? Who was hurt? The shadows in the water kept their secrets.

"Geirr has Lukas by the throat," Filip said, as he sloshed over. He sounded exhausted. "Lukas is vicious."

"Yeah," said Christoffer, slinging his arm around Filip's neck. "Nori is pretty tough, too."

"Apparently they retain their fox teeth," said Filip. "Lukas bit Geirr pretty badly."

"Oh no!" Zaria cried.

"That explains the blood," said Hector as he gripped Christoffer's shoulder and casually reached into his pocket.

Zaria heard a click. Christoffer and Filip looked up at Hector, having heard it too.

"What was that?" she asked, wondering if it was the stargazer she had heard.

"Non-personal magic," Hector whispered out of the side of his mouth. "Act normally all of you."

Zaria quelled the urge to look around, feeling guilty, but only just. After all, non-personal magic wasn't forbidden by the rules… it just wasn't particularly sporting. Christoffer began to look, but Zaria elbowed him.

"Ouch. You and your pointy elbows," he complained. "Be nice."

Hector sighed, "Now we wait."

And so they waited. A steady stream of tiny bubbles burbled up from below. Zaria counted her breaths and it seemed as if time slowed; which she guessed in one respect it had, but not for her. When Lukas broke the surface with a rage-filled yell Zaria couldn't contain herself. She shrieked in joy, jumping up and down.

"Geirr won, Geirr won!" she shouted, grabbing Filip's and Christoffer's hands and doing a merry jig.

"To be on the safe side, he should hold his breath for another few seconds, yes?" Hector asked.

Christoffer nodded. "At least. Maybe thirty."

"I bit his arm pretty good," Lukas growled, having overheard. He dragged himself from the water and said smugly, "He won't be able to last ten seconds let alone thirty. We win, Princess. Give up."

"You're the worst of them," Zaria hissed. "How could you?"

Lukas smiled; his pointy teeth bloody. "I'll take that as a compliment, runt."

She suppressed the urge to panic, as Hector reached for the stargazer hidden in his pocket. He knew what he was doing. She was almost certain of it. When it clicked, Geirr came to the surface, floating facedown. He didn't move. Seeing him, something snapped in Zaria and she started running.

"Geirr," she shouted. "We have to help him!"

The boys dashed into the sea to pull Geirr out. Ignoring the cold, Zaria plunged ahead and grabbed his feet, helping to turn him over. When his face broke the surface, Geirr took deep breaths. He looked dazed and a bit unfocused. As they carried him to the shore he stumbled twice and had to be righted. The shadowy flicker by the water's edge flitted across her vision again. Zaria looked over, but didn't see what it was.

The foxes around the crowd barked and howled, agitated and upset at the loss. The fey grumbled, their voices rising to a dull roar. Zaria, ignoring them, ripped a piece of fabric from Filip's shirt, and used it to bind Geirr's bite wounds.

"You could have used Geirr's shirt you know," Filip complained, fingering the torn hemline of his shirt.

"Don't be a baby, Baby," Geirr muttered, exhausted. "You've got other shirts."

"What if this one had been my favorite?"

"Then I'd say your taste in fashion is poor," Geirr said laughing, but it was weak. He was clearly worn out.

Zaria looked up after tying the last knot and saw the crowds. She did not like the vicious looks aimed at them. She shifted closer to her friends, as Grimkell clapped and raised his hands. Silence descended like a weight, compressing with force on her chest and ears. She felt underwater in the deadened quiet.

"Our friends are now tied with us, but do not fret. They still have more entertainment to provide us. Clear a space; we shall host the tug-o-war here on the shore."

Hector swept off his cloak and tossed it on his bag. He stretched and flexed, dancing on the balls of his feet as he got loose. Like Zaria, Hector knew he was the best choice to compete in the last challenge. Of them, who had more strength?

"Prince Hector, what are you doing?" Nori laughed, sounding like her normal smug self again, although a tightness in her eyes lingered.

"He's my champion for the final competition," Zaria said.

"Can he do that?" Nori questioned her father.

Grimkell fingered his temple, ignoring his daughter. He looked between Aski and Hector as if determining the matchup. A nameless fey with angry eyes handed Grimkell a loop of rope which he accepted. Inspecting it keenly for a moment, he nodded his approval and passed it to Zaria. Hector held out his hand, but Grimkell stayed him.

"No, Stag Lord. The Princess and I agreed to the terms. The Princess and I call our champions. You do not speak for her. Zaria will inspect the rope and deem if it's worthy."

Hector harrumphed and crossed his arms.

"What do I need to look for Hector?" she asked him, quietly on the side.

"Magic," Hector replied. "Because if the rope has any, you should refuse it and demand a plain rope."

Zaria peered at the rope, angling her head this way and that. She closed her eyes trying to sense if

174

anything magical leaked from the rope. All she felt were the coarse scratchy fibers.

She smelled it, afraid of looking silly – the action indeed set off Lukas and Nori, who both laughed cruelly – but she didn't know what to expect. Did magic have a scent? What about flavor? Even if it did, she wouldn't taste it and give them something else to laugh at.

"How would I know if there's magic?" she asked, frustrated. "I've never done this before."

"You'll sense it, Princess. It's part of you."

Zaria held the rope and concentrated. Her eyes crossed, her brows scrunched, and her mouth pursed. Nothing. Zaria shook her head.

"I'm not getting anything."

"Then you approve?" Grimkell asked with a saccharine smile.

Zaria distrusted that look immensely, but she couldn't accuse the rope of being magical. She nodded and handed the rope to Hector. She watched his face to see if she'd made a mistake. His expression didn't change. She breathed a sigh of relief.

"Aski, do us the honors," Grimkell said, waving the fairy into the ring.

Aski and Hector shook hands and settled on the ground. The fairy was shorter than Hector, who had a hand-span in leg-length on him. The rope was arranged with each competitor gathering two handfuls of it. They pressed their feet together, knees bent, and waited.

The crowd, the competitors, and the children held their collective breath. Then the signal was given, and like a rubber band snapping, the silence broke. The crowd of fey and foxes began cheering, barking, jeering, and hollering as both opponents pulled on the rope.

It was an impressive display of strength. Muscles bunched, trembled, and bulged. Aski had more to his wiry form than first glance revealed. He was lean, powerful, and ferocious. If he could help it, Aski would not lose.

Hector by comparison was muscular, brawny, and fit. His chest stretched his shirt taut, and his brows locked together in concentration. Looking at them, you would pick Hector to win, but Aski was making Hector sweat. Zaria could see perspiration form on Hector's brow.

"It looks like rowing," Filip said, as they watched. "Unlike rowing, though, you can't let up, or your opponent tosses you and you lose."

"Hector's got to win," Zaria said. "He's just got to."

Christoffer laughed and gave her a goodhearted shove. He said, "Have you seen the muscles on Hector? Even his muscles have muscles. No way he loses."

"Yeah," Geirr concurred. "No way he loses."

Aski grunted and tilted forward, he came off the ground by a hairsbreadth. Zaria clung to Filip and Christoffer's hands and squeezed hard. Was this it? Was Hector about to throw Aski?

"Ow," Christoffer complained, shaking his hand loose. "You got a heck of a death grip, Princess."

Zaria ignored him, hoping Hector would get the momentum to toss Aski. He didn't. She gasped as Aski threw his weight backward and dropped heavily to the ground. Hector grunted slanting forward at the unexpected recovery. He quickly gathered his wits and pulled.

It was too intense to watch. She could hardly stand it. Zaria covered her eyes with the hand Christoffer let go of and peeked unsteadily between her fingers. Filip gave her a reassuring squeeze. They watched as Aski raised Hector by an inch. Zaria gasped again and hid behind her fingers.

Seconds later, Filip said, "It's okay, Hector recovered."

When Zaria looked again, she sighed in relief. The two opponents were too evenly matched. Hector and Aski were covered in sweat, their grunts were now near constant growls, and their muscles strained mightily to keep up the same level of tension. Neither would let go.

Cords of tension rippled along Hector's neck and arms. With a mighty roar, Hector snapped his legs straight, yanked with all his might and tugged Aski off the ground. In the space of a single heartbeat, leaning backwards as far back as he could go, almost reaching the ground, Hector tossed Aski over his head.

Zaria and her friends raced toward Hector even before the fairy landed in a heap on the ground, moaning. Hector breathed heavily, holding a hand up to stop the children from shouting and cheering, but they ignored it and yammered on excitedly, talking over each other.

Filip said, "You did it, mate!"

"We won, we won," Zaria shouted.

Geirr laughed and said, "You were brilliant."

Christoffer asked, "Was the rope really okay? How are your hands? Do you need help up?"

In the background Grimkell howled frightfully. Winds picked up, blowing Zaria's hair every which way. The friends stopped talking and looked over to where the fairy stood. From inside a furious whirlwind Grimkell pointed an accusing finger at Zaria.

"You cheated," he shouted, gray eyes blazing like lightning. "The agreement is void. Put them in the runt shackles."

"I did not cheat," Zaria said indignantly.

"Your champion, Prince Hector. Ask him. He removed the magic from the rope."

"So you admit to cheating," Hector said, using Geirr's shoulder to pull himself up. The boy nearly toppled under the weight. "An enchanted rope is not fair play."

"Princess Zaria approved it, and it wasn't personal magic. It was allowed. However, I did not approve changes to the rope."

Zaria's brows pulled together. "There wasn't any magic," she said, looking to Hector. "I couldn't feel any."

"That's because you're untrained," Grimkell snarled. "You're pathetic – a worthless heir to the throne, if I ever saw one. If you were mine I would disown you in a heartbeat."

"Like I was disowned?" Aleks asked, appearing beside the group of friends. His hair and clothes were damp. "I'd say hello, Dad, but I wouldn't claim you as family even under torture."

Zaria gasped, "Aleks, no! What are you doing here?"

"Wait – dad?" Filip said, looking from Grimkell to Aleks. "I don't see any resemblance."

"Look closer," Aleks said, crossing his arms over his chest.

"Filthy, changeling," barked Nori, storming over. She planted a fingernail in his chest, poking him with every word. "You. Do. Not. Speak."

"Sis," Aleks said, dryly. "I've been observing you from a distance today. Your filial loyalty is quite lacking, isn't it?"

"You are not my family," she said imperiously, rising to her full height above him.

"You made sure of that," Aleks said calmly. "You convinced Lord Grimkell I was a threat, didn't you? But the real question is: a threat to whom?"

She waved away his accusation. "You are not a threat to anyone, you ugly thing."

"He's not ugly," Zaria interjected hotly. "He's better than all of you!"

"Son," Grimkell acknowledged. "Didn't my aunt warn you about returning to Niffleheim? Changelings do not live long here."

Aleks raised a brow. "No, I don't suspect they do, but that doesn't matter. You can't do anything to harm me."

Lukas shoved his way into the circle, magic crackling in his fingers. "That's where you're wrong, little brother. I'm going to end your pitiful existence right now."

"You can't," Hector said, his tone jovial and a touch gloating. "He's with us, and we've won safe passage into Jerndor."

"How did you get down here?" Lukas demanded. "We would have sensed you immediately."

"I think you did," Aleks said with a smirk. "But you ignored me, captured my friends, and went on your merry way. Hector and I spied on you from a distance, until you disappeared in the palace. Hector and I then tested a theory. To all fey I was invisible."

"Not quite," Hector replied, "but nearly so. As long as you didn't talk, or touch them, they ignored you. One of your guards is tied up in some alleyway somewhere in the city."

Aleks grinned and said, "Right. Once that was sorted out, I strolled into the palace and found my friends. I overheard the challenge being issued between Grimkell and Zaria from the hallway outside the Great Fox Hall. I stayed long enough to know where to be for the second challenge and left, walking out through the front door. Not once did you notice me."

"How," Lukas demanded. "How can that be? You're not that powerful. Your human family has stripped you of most of your magic."

"Zaria gave him protection," Hector revealed.

Surprised, she said, "I did? When?"

"At the well," Hector replied. "I think it had to do with your wish."

"The well granted my wish didn't it?" she asked in wonder. "I prayed for Aleks' safety. Wished for it too."

"And it was granted, twice over," Hector said. "Once by hiding him until he made his presence known, and again, I think, with the rope. You missed it Princess, but the rope did have magic in it. I could sense it from a distance, but I didn't know what it was. By the time you handed it to me though, the magic was gone, even though you didn't use magic to accomplish its removal."

"You think it was the well in both instances?" Christoffer asked. He whistled. "That's awesome."

Hector nodded, "Yes, I do. Because Aleks' ultimate fate rested with the outcome of the challenges, I think the well ensured that Zaria's team won."

Nori stamped her foot. "That is cheating!"

"Ah-ah," Hector countered, waving a finger. "Not according to the rules your father and Zaria agreed to. No personal magic was allowed, yes, but I do believe nobody present would claim that the Lost Well is Zaria's personal magic."

Grimkell slashed a hand to the side, scattering his subjects. The ground erupted in violence where they'd been standing. He gave a grudging nod of respect.

He admitted, "I can't even aim my hand at the changeling. Very well. It is time we honor the terms of the competition."

"But Father," protested Lukas and Nori at once. "You can't!"

Nori added, "The changeling must be punished for his return. He must be killed. What would the other courts think, if we were to let him go? They would think us weak. It would be political suicide to let him escape retribution."

"They would converge on us to steal back the crown and scepter," Lukas said.

"We will prepare for that when the time comes," Grimkell said with ice. "In the meantime, we will not dishonor the Autumn House by reneging on a deal. That, as you both know, is worse than a changeling in our midst."

They both looked like they wanted to argue further, but Grimkell silenced them with a current of angry magic. They subsided and meekly fell into place behind their father. Lukas glared at Aleks with thinly veiled hate. Nori however pierced Zaria with her glittery gaze, and Zaria knew that if looks could kill, she would die where she stood.

Chapter Eleven: The Specter in the Dark

Grimkell deposited the group deep in the bowels of Niffleheim. They had climbed down a steep, dank, loamy trail, and waded through muck to get where they were. Hector stood beside Grimkell, legs braced apart, as he surveyed the darkened doorway. The way was unlit; the door hanging by its hinges, as if something massive had broken it.

"I thought the fey would block this off," Hector said, studying Grimkell's profile. "Why would you leave the Thief of Peace's Passage unblocked and unguarded? This is how Fritjof entered into your kingdom and decimated your people, leaving chaos in his wake."

Grimkell's eyes glowed yellow in the dim light, as he assessed them. "To remind the fey that even our allies can be more treacherous than our enemies. We might have been freed of a dragon menace, but we lost something much more valuable to us, when you hid our well and cut us off from our source of magic."

Lukas smiled nastily, gesturing to the passageway. "The way is perfectly safe, if you're worried. When the ellefolken and elves trapped Koll's youngest brother in the Under Realm, this became a harmless passageway into Niffleheim from Jerndor. The dwarves even lined it with mirrors to protect it."

"Mirrors?" squeaked Zaria, discomfited by the idea. She did not want to be around reflective surfaces.

"The grand mirror at the end will be your entrance into Jerndor," Grimkell explained. "The dwarves enchanted the mirror to be a gateway between our kingdoms."

Hector reached a hand out to Grimkell. "Farewell, Lord Grimkell. I hope we can match wits again."

Grimkell shook Hector's hand and withdrew. "Don't be offended when I say, I don't. Farewell, Stag Lord." He turned to stare at Zaria. "Farewell, Princess. You, of course, are welcome to return. We have much to discuss."

"About the well?" she guessed.

"Precisely. You made a wish on it, and it granted it to you. The well doesn't always do that. You have powerful magic in you. I see great potential in that."

"You'd better run along now," Nori said with a disdainful sniff. Zaria hadn't missed that obnoxious flourish.

"The passage closes on our end at dawn – in a few moments," Lukas added. "Good-bye, little brother; you won't be missed."

Aleks flipped him a rude gesture and marched to the crooked door. He wedged it open with force – Hector helped – and slipped inside. Hector pried the door open further. At the movement, the hinges protested loudly. Zaria followed Geirr with Christoffer and Filip right behind her, as the last echoes of it faded.

"We got out of that pickle relatively easily," Christoffer said, when the door vanished, leaving a dirt wall in its place. Hector handed out flashlights.

"I beg to differ," Geirr said, rubbing his bandaged arm. "I didn't like being almost drowned."

"Why are you complaining? I was underwater, trapped in a bubble for days, while you guys went on an adventure last time. You only had to spend a few minutes underwater. No big deal."

"Yeah, well, at least you could breathe. Oh, hey," Geirr said, as he gave Aleks a small shove. "I sort of remember you appearing in the lake. What happened?"

"I froze time," Hector said. He motioned with his flashlight for the kids to start walking. "At first, I wasn't sure about the plan. You know ellefolken don't like to mess with time, but Aleks convinced me it was the only way to win. We deactivated it before going to the sea. I was to distract the fey and reactivate the stargazer, while Aleks ensured Geirr stayed under for as long as was needed, so we would win."

"Then that's why your hair and clothes were damp!" Christoffer exclaimed, clapping Aleks on the back in appreciation. "Good job! If Geirr had surfaced any sooner, we would've lost. But how were you in the water? How did you both stay under?"

Aleks scratched the back of his neck, remembering. "Well, I slipped into the water just as Isak and Filip came to the surface."

"Oh," Zaria interrupted. "I think I saw you do that. I didn't look up in time to actually see you, but I saw the water move over where you'd been."

Aleks nodded. "I found Geirr and Lukas. Geirr had Lukas in a stranglehold. They were struggling. I was a bit nervous that I'd reveal myself by accident to Lukas as I got closer, but I managed to evade Lukas and grab Geirr's foot. You almost kicked me in the face by the way, not cool.

"Then I grabbed a boulder on the seafloor, and Hector restarted the stargazer, putting us both in stasis. I'm not sure what Lukas thought, but seeing that we won, he must've needed to breathe and freed himself from Geirr's hold so he could go to the surface."

"Will turning the stargazer off and on and off again affect time back home?" Filip asked, biting his lip. "Mum wasn't very happy when I left."

Hector nodded grimly. "I guess that it would. There isn't much we can do about it now. The circumstances made turning the stargazer off and on necessary."

"We aren't in Fredrikstad to reactivate it," Filip said. "If our parents are unfrozen, what are they going to think when they find us gone?"

"I hadn't thought about that," Zaria said, worried. "Mom and Papa are going to be super upset."

Christoffer groaned. "You think *your* parents are going to be upset? Mine will never let me leave the house again!"

"Not until you're fifty-five and married," Aleks said jokingly, before shrugging and adding, "I think Grams will cover for me. She'll figure it out. After all, having an adventure is why she gave me the stargazer in the first place."

Geirr said, "At least it's summer. Can you imagine if we were gone in the middle of the school year?"

"I think we're all doomed," Filip said glumly. He kicked at a pebble, sending it skittering across the floor.

The group walked in silence for a while, contemplating the punishments that awaited them when the adventure was over. It was a worry, but the bigger picture fortified Zaria's resolve to keep going. Hart needed to be rescued and reunited with his father. She looked at Hector's determined visage and knew she would do all in her power to see that the happy event happened.

"I'm glad these mirrors are coated in dirt," Filip said, waving his flashlight along the walls. "The fey have too many reflective surfaces."

Zaria gave a hum of agreement as she waved her flashlight over the mirrors. A shadow skittered to her right. Startled, she swung the flashlight over to it. Her breath caught. The terror that haunted her was back.

"Did anyone see that?" she asked nervously.

Flashlight beams joined at hers, illuminating the corridor. Zaria saw it slip ahead. She jerked her beam to the left. The others copied her. The shadow was gone.

"I don't see anything," Aleks said. "What was it?"

"A figure," Zaria said. "I'm sure of it. Didn't any of you see it?"

She looked at them and each of her friends shook their head. She looked to Hector, pleading with her eyes for him to back her up. He too shook his head.

"Princess, I don't sense anything down here. It's only us."

Just then Zaria felt fingers run up her back. She shrieked and leapt forward, dropping her flashlight. It clattered to the ground, casting its light wildly across their feet.

"S-s-something touched me!" she stammered.

Aleks stooped to pick up the flashlight. He handed it to her. "Zaria, there's nothing here."

"There is," she cried. "Please believe me."

The boys looked to Hector, who methodically searched the darkness around them. He frowned deeply as he looked for the thing that haunted her. Eventually he dropped the light.

"Are you certain you felt something?" Geirr asked. He laid a kind hand on her shoulder. "You can walk between us. Aleks and I can take the outer edges."

"We should keep moving," Hector said, motioning for everyone to step closer to the center. "Everyone flank Zaria. If there is something here, she'll be protected."

The boys took the responsibility seriously. Aleks and Geirr flanked her left side, Christoffer her right, Filip at the front, and Hector guarded the rear. Zaria was embarrassed by all the fuss. She felt like a loser. She hugged herself and stared at her feet.

Christoffer gave her a playful nudge. "Why such a sad face?"

"It's too much," she said, stifling a sob, which made her hiccup. She covered her face with her hand. "You guys don't have to do this."

"Sure we do," Aleks said, giving her a one-armed hug. "We protect each other. It's what we do."

"We won't let some ghostie or whatever get you," Christoffer said, puffing out his chest.

"There's no such thing as ghosts," Zaria said. At the same time Hector echoed, "Ghosts aren't real."

Filip looked over his shoulder. "I think we should be more worried about dragons. This Fritjof character sounds like bad news."

"You are correct," Hector replied. "He's trapped with his brothers in the Under Realm."

"Who's the third brother?" Geirr asked. "We know of Koll and Fritjof."

"Bjarke's crew mentioned Egil," Zaria said, remembering the story of how that dragon almost poisoned the river-troll.

Hector said, "Yes, Egil, is the middle brother. The only thing worse than Koll being set free is if all three brothers are mistakenly set free by this crazy plan of Olaf's."

Geirr flicked his flashlight over the mirrors. "Why is that?"

"Separate they're bad enough, together they're nigh unstoppable. They were captured the last time out of sheer luck. They hate each other as much as they hate everyone else. If they were to get loose, I think we might find them working together."

Filip looked back at Hector. "Wouldn't Olaf want all three out?"

"No," Hector said immediately. "He would not be so foolish. One dragon might bargain for freedom and honor the agreement. Two or more would play mind games, until it amused them more for Olaf to be dead than alive. Olaf values his life."

"What makes them unstoppable?" Zaria asked in a soft voice. "I mean, together, because obviously they're pretty dangerous on their own."

Hector touched her shoulder briefly. "They're the trifecta of evil incarnate: darkness, fear, and chaos. Their powers would feed off each other and grow into something massive and uncontrollable."

"We're here," Filip announced, stopping. He pointed his flashlight at the large silver mirror before them. "What now?"

"Trade spots with me," Hector said, pushing forward.

Filip took his place at the rear. He gave Zaria a small smile, touching her fingers as he went by. She tangled her fingers with his briefly and let go.

Hector swiped a hand over the mirror, clearing off a circle of dust. Geirr wrinkled his nose as dust lifted from the mirror and swirled around them. Hector braced his hands on the grimy ornate frame and peered into the mirror.

"Mirror, mirror, on the wall," joked Christoffer, giving her a wink.

Zaria rolled her eyes at him. "Ha, ha, very funny."

The mirror rippled like moving water, scattering the dust and dirt. It rained down on them. Zaria threw her arms over her head, trying to keep the debris out of her hair. Aleks brushed off a layer that had settled on his shoulders and shook his head, sending out another flurry of dust. Through it all, Hector didn't seem to notice them. He was staring intently into the mirror.

"Uh, Hector," Aleks said hesitantly. "What are you doing?"

When he didn't respond, the children shuffled nervously. It was as if Hector wasn't present, which was impossible, because he clearly was. They could see him.

Aleks poked their Stag Lord friend in the shoulder. A full minute passed before Hector moved. He staggered away from the mirror and glared at it furiously.

"What's wrong?" Geirr asked.

"The guards won't let us through until this afternoon."

"Why not?" Zaria wondered.

Hector furrowed his fingers in his hair. "They said it was a precaution against anything traveling through the mirror with us. Each delay costs us. We must get the sword."

"We will," Aleks promised. "We'll free Hart, too. Look at it this way, we're not having to trade with giants for a proper introduction anymore."

"Might still have been faster," Hector said with a sigh, sinking against the wall. "Since we have no introductions, the guards can still deny us entry later today."

"Oh no," Zaria said. She slipped from between the boys and crouched before Hector. "Will they really do that?"

He ran a hand down his face and closed his eyes. "They might."

Filip looked to Aleks. "Do you have food in your bag? I'm famished, and we lost our stuff when the fey captured us."

Hector sat up and pulled his bag over. He unclipped another bag hanging from his and passed it to Zaria.

"Zaria's was the only one light enough to carry easily," he said apologetically to the boys. "We had to abandon the tents too."

Next, he freed Madam Brown. As she grew back to her normal height, he gave her a tired smile. "Madam Brown, would you make us something to eat? You are a marvelous cook, and we are short on supplies and are very hungry."

"Of course," she squeaked. "I know just what to do."

The brownie then proceeded to make a feast out of what little supplies remained. The smells unleashed a tidal wave of hunger in Zaria, and she scarfed down the hot stew and salty jerky, caring little when it burnt the roof of her mouth. The boys followed suit, and with gusty sighs, they all fell into a food coma having stuffed themselves to the gills.

***

Zaria awoke sometime later, her heart knocking wildly in her chest. Fear clogged her throat, and she didn't know why. The embers of the fire Madam Brown and Filip had started from pieces of fallen and broken timber were all but burnt out. A dim glowing red snuggled in its heart was all that remained. She couldn't see anything in the gloom.

Her ragged breathing was so loud to Zaria's ears, she was sure it called attention to her wakefulness. Something was watching her. It could see her in the darkness. She knew it, as surely as she knew the others were fast asleep. Filip's snores told her so.

Zaria licked her lips and tried to quiet her harsh breathing. Her eyes slowly adjusted in the dark. She vaguely saw the forms of her sleeping friends around the fire. As nothing moved and nothing happened, Zaria's heartbeat slowed. The fear dislodged and she began to relax, melting back toward sleep.

As she was about to slip under, a cold hand passed over her brow and foul breath filled her nostrils.

"Wakey, wakey, Princess," the terror from her dreams said.

Zaria screamed – or she tried to – but the cold hand clamped down over her mouth.

"Now, now, Princess, try not to wake yer little friends. We wouldn't want them hurt, now would we?"

It leaned closer, and Zaria squeezed her eyes shut, and whimpered. It laughed and the sound raised the hair on her arms and legs, freezing her in place.

"Yer terror is delicious," the specter said, as it sniffed the air loudly before sighing with wicked enjoyment. "So tasty. It makes the air crackle. Can ye feel it?"

Zaria shook her head beneath the hand holding her.

"No? Pity. Or not," it said, cackling at a secret joke, before sobering abruptly. "I plan to follow ye everywhere, Princess, be yer shadow. Then one day, when I've eaten enough of yer terror, I will become ye. Surely, ye've seen the resemblance."

She squeaked.

"How will I do it?" the trollish nightmare asked, guessing what she said. Its hair swung forward in heavy braids, tickling her forehead. "Never mind how, but ye go right on ahead and keep looking over yer shoulder. It'll make the process go much faster. It's nearly complete as it is. Yer such a fearful little thing. Not brave at all."

Her heart quaked at the words. They felt so real. The truth of them weighed her down, sinking her unspoken hope. When it licked her skin, she squealed, thrashing under it.

The figure leapt back, laughing again its horrible laugh. "Try to get some sleep, Princess, I plan to haunt yer dreams – waking and sleeping."

Zaria stayed awake all night, hugging herself and hating herself for it, fearful that above all, her actions even now were hastening the reappearance of the terrible trollish specter with its gleaming yellow and purple eyes.

She must have dozed off eventually, for Zaria suddenly startled awake. Once more her heart hammered in her throat, as she looked wildly around.

The fire had been covered in dirt and a ring of eerily lit faces peered down at her.

"Take it easy," Christoffer chided, swinging his flashlight away from his face and giving her a hand up. "We're about to go through the portal. Hector's secured us passage after another round of mirror talk."

Filip handed her a cup of water. She drank it greedily. "You all right?" he asked.

She nodded and handed him back the cup. "Fine," she said tightly, hugging her arms. "I'm fine."

"Ready to go children?" Hector called out. "It's time."

"Could I go first?" Zaria asked, eager to get out of the mirrored hallway and away from the specter's taunting presence.

"Of course," Hector said, holding out his hand. "Mirror travel is easy enough. Once you start, simply keep pushing through. It'll feel like dry water."

"Dry water? Isn't that an oxymoron?" Aleks said wryly.

Hector shrugged, offering a wan smile. "Step through, and then tell me what you think it feels like."

Aleks held up his hands in surrender. "Okay, sure, dry water, whatever you say."

Zaria gave her hand to Hector, and he guided her through the mirror. It was cool, wet, and treacly but her skin never dampened. Dry water. Or maybe dry syrup. It sucked her in and pushed her out, before she could even latch onto the sensation of mirror traveling beyond that first superficial impression.

She slipped out the other side into a gray stone corridor. Waiting for her were half a dozen cloaked dwarf guards with sharp and gleaming weapons. Zaria swallowed and raised her hands in surrender.

Timidly, she said, "I come in peace."

Chapter Twelve: A Tale of Two Fathers

Zaria assumed Hector would be livid at their treatment by the dwarves, but he merely nodded his head in greeting and began to address the head guard.

"Quite the welcome committee," Christoffer said, looking around. "Do you think they do this for everyone or are we just special?"

"We're probably just special," Aleks said, scratching his nose. He looked more relaxed than he should have been with weapons aimed at him. "I'm glad to be out of Niffleheim territory."

"Me too," Geirr said, rubbing his arms in the chill of the corridor. "They're not very hospitable."

"That's an understatement," Filip chortled.

Aleks shrugged. "I'm glad I wasn't killed."

"Me too," Filip said bumping shoulders with him. "Can't picture you without a head, mate. Although you might be prettier than you are now."

Aleks laughed weakly and touched his throat. "Ha. Ha. I like my head where it is just fine. Thanks, Zaria. If it wasn't for your wish at the well, I'd be a goner for sure."

"No problem," she said with a distracted smile. "Team effort. If you hadn't caught up with Hector and arrived when you did, we'd have been toast."

Hector stomped over, wrapping his cloak tighter around himself. "They're taking us to the waiting chamber before we meet King Flein. Dwarvish customs say we could be waiting for an audience with him for up to two weeks, but I think I've managed to convince the guard the importance of the visitation and the importance of the visitors."

"Yeah, two weeks isn't ideal," Christoffer said. "If the stargazer is turned off back home, and Mum and Dad realize I'm gone, they will blow a gasket."

Hector nodded. "All of your parents would be upset, and even if by some miracle it held, Hart can't wait that long. The power in the chains comes from this bedrock with its special ore. It's oppressive and draining. Hart is not a dragon, and time is not his friend. He could be killed."

"Killed?" Zaria said numbly. "You mean what I did could get him killed?"

Hector shook his head. "Don't take upon yourself the sins of another. Olaf is to blame. Now we must go. Stay close and no wandering off. The way seems unremarkable, but it is easy to lose oneself in these halls."

They followed the dwarves through large gray corridors. Gems twinkled around doorways as they went through cross sections. Everything appeared to be cut and squared, precisely measured. Despite the similarities to the totalitarian world of the fey, it was an altogether different feel, like a quaint medieval village. Dwarvish architecture was exact, but homey in a way. Maybe it was the earthen flooring or the warm light from the torches.

As they crossed one hallway, Zaria looked to her left and saw to her amazement dwarf children running around playing games, ducking through their mothers' hanging laundry, as the women chatted. They were happy and carefree, completely unconcerned by the company of guards and strangers marching through their midst.

Down another corridor it looked like a shopping district. The winding alley featured large and small old-fashioned signs, indicating their stores' contents. There was the Mighty Hollows, a weapons shop, the Red Dwarf Fashion Emporium, and even Small and Tall Tales, a book shop. All signs displayed wealth, each one encrusted with twinkling gems and sprinkled liberally with gold leaf.

Zaria peered into windows and doors, fascinated and tingly with the urge to shop. It seemed to her that the maze of crisscrossing hallways was actually city streets. All of the homes and businesses were built into the walls. Nothing was freestanding, except for the fountains in courtyards, tinkling musically in the cultivated gloom.

As they walked the streets, they would be blown with sharp cold air. On a particularly chilly blast, Zaria looked up, and saw a hole cut in the ceiling.

"Fresh air shafts," Hector informed her, seeing her look up.

Next they passed what must be a church with its colored glass and fancy window panes. Zaria could make out the fanciful designs, because the church was lit from within. It had a large, ornate, iron door with a worn teal patina, a color only achieved by the march of time.

They rounded one last corner, and the bustling streets ended. The hall narrowed, and at its end was a plain, unmarked wood door. Their guards dropped away, leaving them in the company of the head guard. He opened the plain door without flourish and ushered them inside.

On the other side of the door was a medium-sized room with a pit in the middle and stone benches lined all around the edges. Milling around the room were many dwarves, a handful of elves, a couple of mountain-trolls, and even a giant. Some of them were standing down in the pit talking quietly among themselves.

The giant, thankfully, wasn't as large as their friend Ingdor the Thunderous. He looked younger than their friend too. Perhaps he was a teenager. The markings on his skin were different in color than the Seiland giants. Zaria thought that might indicate which bedrock he formed from.

"Wait here," the dwarf commanded. "You'll be summoned when either Prince Floki or King Flein is ready to hear your petition."

Hector, whose antler cloak was wrapped regally around his shoulders, gave the dwarf a steely look. "Make haste to inform their majesties that the Stag Lord of Elleken and Princess Zaria of the Under Realm are here for an audience. Do not delay in the telling."

"Of course," the dwarf said silkily, his expression condescending. Then he shut the door on them and was gone.

"That was very imperious and royal of you," Christoffer remarked. "This room is interesting. What do you think the pit is for?"

"Executions," Hector said brusquely. Then he stomped over to the benches lining the walls.

Zaria hurried after him. "I don't think I heard you right. Did you say –"

"Executions? Yes, I did."

"But from, like the Viking era, right? The dwarves don't hold executions anymore, do they? It'd be barbaric."

"You'd be surprised by how barbaric they can be, Princess," he said, settling on the bench and leaning back against the wall. "You might want to rest. Despite the command for haste, we will probably be here a while."

Aleks settled on the dirt floor and looked around the room. "So is this waiting area really where we wait for an audience with King Flein, or is this where we wait to be executed?"

"It can be both places at the same time," Hector said, opening his pack and handing the children dried fruit. "Go on, eat. This is not a time for empty stomachs. We must have our wits about us."

So, they sat and ate, and the hours went by interminably. To pass the time, Christoffer made friends with the giant. Pekka the Overwhelming was decidedly underwhelming. He spoke at length about his hobby, which was rabbit farming. Pekka explained in great detail how he chose their names, and described their personalities and markings. Christoffer's eyes glazed over after the first sentence, and he couldn't extract himself fast enough from the conversation.

The most interesting thing Pekka had to say concerned his occupation. It turned out that he was there as an official messenger between Rjupa the Bountiful and King Flein. When Hector prompted him for the news, they learned that the hags and their wolverines were no longer a threat to Stabbursdalen, but that humans had noticed something strange in the area and were on alert.

"That is good news," Hector said, pulling the young giant aside to discuss it and press for other news.

"I'm bored," Filip said. "I hate waiting."

"We're all bored," Geirr replied, rolling his eyes. "I'd kill for a book. Zaria did you bring any with you? You are always carrying one around."

Zaria nodded and pulled out a well-worn book. "I got this book for my last birthday," she said, handing it to Geirr. "It's about a boy who learns he can control lightning."

"Like Zeus from Greek mythology?"

"Well, not exactly. He isn't Greek. It takes place in Australia and he –"

"Princess Zaria, Stag Lord, their majesties await your presence in the receiving chamber."

Zaria shrugged and put the book away. "Maybe another time, but the trilogy is really good. I'm sure you'd like it."

The receiving chamber was back across the center of town and down another series of corridors. Zaria seriously envied Aleks' innate ability to orient himself and navigate in strange and unfamiliar surroundings.

She gave up trying to remember where she was and focused on the faces of the dwarves peering out at them from behind colorful curtains and multi-paned windows.

As they were escorted into the chamber, a chill swept down Zaria's back. She looked for its source and saw the disappearing figure of her tormentor at the opposite end of the hall. Her heart knew that its appearance here wasn't good.

"Welcome, welcome, Stag Lord," King Flein said, standing up and waving his arms.

Zaria's first impression of the dwarf king was that he had an affable demeanor. As they approached him, he dropped his arms and righted his jewel-encrusted belt over his large stomach. The king watched them with twinkling eyes.

"It's good to meet with you officially this time," King Flein said. "Most surprising indeed, that your appearance came by the Niffleheim mirror. What on earth were you doing there?"

"Finding passage and introduction into your realm," Hector said dryly. "I couldn't get an introduction by other means. Your guards refused me entrance last time I was on the doorstep of your kingdom."

"We are rather protective of our realm," the king said with an unapologetic shrug. "We can't to be too careful with strangers. Olaf is stirring up trouble everywhere. You could have been in league with him."

"Why grant us an audience now?" Hector asked.

"Your story was verified after you left," King Flein shared. "My spies tell me your Golden Kings are falling to rot. That is distressing news. Your forefathers are meant to keep the dragons from seeping out into the world. What do you plan to do about it?"

"I am here with Princess Zaria to claim the Drakeland Sword that was left in your great-grandfather's keeping."

Prince Floki, an exact look-alike of his father, same rotund shape, same bright red beard, laughed boisterously, slapping his knees in delight. Zaria gave him a sour look. What was funny about their request?

"Why should we believe your little human girl is Queen Helena's daughter?" asked Floki.

"Surely the reports you received from your spies –"

"Only verified you," Floki stated, the humor draining from his face. "As she wasn't with you when you came to us months ago, we saw no reason to seek out her story. What does Queen Helena say?"

Hector frowned. "Silje and I haven't been able to contact her in the last six months. Before then, we hadn't tried to reach out to her. We last spoke not quite a year ago."

"That's a pity," King Flein said, with a shake of his head. He returned to his throne and sat down. He rubbed his knees and straightened his crown. "Well, unless you can prove the girl's identity, I'm afraid your journey has been for naught."

Prince Floki waved imperiously toward the back of the room. "Guards, please escort our guests to the visitor corridor." Addressing Hector, he added, "You can rest for the night, but then you must be on your way tomorrow."

Hector was furious. "That's it? You won't even ask why we're requesting the sword? You won't take into account the urgency of the need? You just commented on the rotting of the Golden Kings. You know what that means."

King Flein was no longer the friendly, overweight dwarf. He glowered mightily. "Stag Lord, we've been most generous in granting this audience. Our time is limited, and the needs of our people plentiful. We agreed to meet you because of our deepest respect for Queen Helena.

"She came to my great-grandfather with a crazy plan – a plan to trap the world's dragons in a void built by the best fey realm crafters, rooted in place by the great ellefolken kings of old, who would be relocated inside Gloomwood Forest a few clicks from the Gjöll, guarded by the fiercest elven warriors, and watched over by the greatest sorceress on the earth.

"It was a plan that needed dwarvish metallurgy to craft two very important objects – chains to imprison the dragons and drain them of their fearsome powers and a sword that would be fearless in the presence of dragons. The plan worked, but it wasn't flawless.

"Dragons aren't so easily ensnared. They are driven to escape. They never stop pushing to get back into the world. It was learned that the sword could wound, but couldn't kill the dragons. Still, all the dragons were captured and herded over the Gjallarbrú, chained down and rooted into place. Their powers waned, and we thought we were safe. Only Queen Helena would realize too late that the sword was too dangerous to be kept in the Under Realm."

"Stop!" Hector warned.

"Does the girl not know?"

"It is not your place."

King Flein raised an affronted brow. He looked over to Zaria and said, "Valgard, your father, was slain by the Drakeland Sword during a dragon uprising soon after you were born."

"Is that true?" Zaria asked. She looked to Hector for confirmation.

He crossed his arms and shook his head. "This story is for your mother to tell you."

Prince Floki raised an eyebrow, matching his father's look. "It seems to me she had plenty of time to tell her daughter, if she was going to do so."

"Why was my father killed?" Zaria demanded.

"He got in the way of an enterprising giant, Vella the Vaultless. The dragon Fritjof corrupted her with promises of immortality. She freed the sword from its encasement in the Under Realm and used it against your father, when he stood between her and the dragon."

"Why didn't he stop Vella with magic?"

"Valgard wasn't a sorcerer. He was merely human," Hector explained with grief in his eyes. "He was a good friend and very brave. He loved your mother very much and stayed with her in the Under Realm, even though the atmosphere was so toxic."

"So you see," Flein said, gently, resuming a friendlier tone. "We granted an audience out of our deepest respects, but this sword is capable of freeing or felling dragons. This knowledge has made its safekeeping even more vital than our kingdom's fresh air shafts. We will not be responsible for the next Vella the Vaultless. You have twenty-four hours to prove yourself to be Queen Helena's daughter. Then you must leave."

Zaria looked around the room at her friends, the dwarf rulers, Hector, and the nearby guards. The room was suddenly suffocating. Her eyes welled with tears, as she thought about the story she'd just heard.

"I – I can't breathe," she stammered. "I must go."

"Zaria, wait!" Hector said, crossing the room toward her, hand outstretched.

She didn't wait. Instead, she ran for the doors and pushed through them blindly, stumbling down corridor after corridor. Lost and alone she sank against a rough wall and cried her heart out, missing a father, who loved her and whom she never knew, and a father who loved her and was surely sick with worry, missing her back home.

***

"Are you okay, Zar-Zar?" Filip asked, stepping into her guest room. "You were quiet at dinner."

Zaria shrugged, tucking her hands between her knees. "I know. I am all mixed-up. My emotions are all over the place."

"So let's un-mix them," he said, sitting next to her on the bed.

Zaria laughed weakly. "Yeah, okay." She bumped her shoulder against his.

He nudged her back. "You're sad," he said simply, watching her. "You suddenly miss someone you don't even remember."

She nodded.

"And you're worried about your parents back home, what they're thinking and feeling."

She nodded again.

"And you want to rescue Hart. You think it's all your fault he's trapped and hurting somewhere."

She leaned her head against his shoulder, not saying anything. Filip wrapped an arm around her, and rested his chin against her hair.

"You're wrong, you know," he said. "Olaf is the bad guy. He's scheming and devious. He's responsible for this whole mess, not you. Even if you don't believe it."

Zaria kept quiet. She couldn't explain it, but she felt she knew deep down that it was all her fault. Even somehow her birth father's death was because of her. Logically, she knew from the dwarves and Hector that it wasn't her fault. But why would her mother give her up? Why would she never reach out to find her?

Filip rubbed her arms and said, "We'll rescue Hart like we rescued Christoffer."

As if he heard them talking about him, Christoffer appeared in the doorway. He knocked lightly on the door jamb and stepped inside. "Filip giving you a pep talk?" he asked, taking a seat on the other side of her.

"Trying to anyway," Filip said.

"You should listen to him," Christoffer said. "Filip's pretty smart... well, sometimes."

"Yeah – hey!" Filip complained.

Christoffer stuck his tongue out at Filip. Looking back to Zaria he said, "You feeling better?"

"A little," she acknowledged. "How am I going to prove who I am? I mean, let's get real. I've never met my birth mother. I don't know who she is or what she even looks like. Hector is certain I'm her daughter, but is it possible he's wrong?"

Christoffer laughed and poked her in the ribs. "Zaria, did you forget the troll that started all this? Olaf went after you and your friends. He sought you out first. That's your endorsement."

"Such as it is," Filip said, rolling his eyes.

Zaria bit her lip. "Okay. So, how can I prove my lineage without these so-called powers that I'm supposed to have, but don't? We'll never get the sword at this rate."

"Never fear," Christoffer said, offering up a cheeky grin. "Aleks had an idea for that."

Just then Aleks stuck his head through the door. His bright ginger hair glowed under the torch-light. "Is that my cue?" he asked.

"Come on, man," Christoffer whined. "You're ruining the drama of the moment."

Zaria laughed as Aleks stepped into the room. He leaned against the wall and put his hands in his pockets. A moment later he pulled out the stargazer and tossed it to Zaria. She caught it on reflex.

"The stargazer?" she queried, looking at the three of them. "What am I supposed to do with this?"

"Well," Aleks said with a smirk. "You stop time with it for one thing –"

"I know that, you goose," Zaria said, making a face.

Filip grabbed the stargazer and waved it under her nose. "Aleks told us that back when we escaped from my mum, you didn't freeze like the rest of us –"

"– and you weren't frozen when Hector used it in Niffleheim at the lake because –" Christoffer continued.

"– you're magical," Aleks concluded. He walked over, plucked the ovoid device from Filip's lax grip and waved it at her. "You're the daughter of Queen Helena, and this little guy here will prove it."

Zaria snatched it from Aleks, hope filling her up full to bursting. "Hector, the dwarves, and I won't freeze because we're magical beings while the three of you will be stopped in your tracks."

"Because we're human," Geirr said, joining the four of them. "Well mostly," he added, nodding at Aleks. He shut the door to the room and leaned against it.

Zaria looked them over one by one, tears of gratitude in her eyes. Their faces blurred, when more tears filled her eyes and overflowed. She wiped them away quickly and ran her sleeve across her nose.

"You guys," she said, a little choked up. "This is going to work!"

She gave each of them a big hug, squeezing them tight. Filip's ears burned red as she let go. The boys said goodnight and went back down the hall to their bedchambers.

Zaria went to sleep feeling positive that the outcome of her meeting with the dwarf king the next day would be successful. She would get the sword for Hector, and then they could find and free Hart. It was all going to work out okay in the end. She just knew it.

Chapter Thirteen:
Acquiring the Sword

King Flein and Prince Floki granted their second hearing sooner than their first, with four hours to spare before the twenty-four hour deadline. Zaria, Hector, and the others had gathered in the receiving chamber. The trollish specter was nowhere to be seen, which gave Zaria no small bit of comfort.

"Greetings, Stag Lord," King Flein said between bites of a large meaty bone. He pointed the food at them. "Are you prepared to prove the girl's lineage?"

Hector nodded. "Without a doubt, your Majesty. Aleks can you give me the device?"

"Excuse me," Prince Floki sneered. "What device? Guards, take it from the boy."

Aleks handed it over to the approaching guard with a shrug. "Suit yourself."

"Bring that here," Floki demanded, snapping his fingers impatiently. Jeweled rings glinted from every one of his fat fingers.

Christoffer and Zaria shared an amused look, before turning to face the dwarves. The prince snatched the stargazer from the guard's hand and began examining it thoroughly. He held it up to the light and peered inside the star-shaped holes.

"What is it, son?" Flein asked before taking another bite and licking his fingers.

"What is it?" Floki asked Aleks.

"It's a stargazer. My grams gave it to me, when she found out I was a changeling."

"A magic trinket from the witch in the woods?" King Flein asked, delighted by the idea. "Let me see it."

Grudgingly, Floki handed it to his father and sat back on his throne. He drummed his fingers along the armrests. "How is this going to prove the girl is the daughter of Queen Helena?"

Flein rolled his eyes at his son. "Honestly, boy, don't your tutors teach you anything? A stargazer stops time. Its side effect is freezing non-magical beings, like humans, in place, when it's activated. If the girl, who looks human, is not stopped by the device, then she isn't human –"

"– which makes her magical," Hector said. "If she is magical, she is then Queen Helena's daughter. None else could she be."

"How does it work?" the king asked eagerly, wiping his hands down his doublet. "Where is the button to turn it on?"

Aleks walked up to the throne and pointed to the largest star. "You click here to turn it on, your Majesty."

"Very good. Stag Lord, do you know the trick to turning it off?"

"I do."

"Excellent," he said and pressed the button.

Aleks froze in place, right next to the dwarf king. Filip, Geirr, and Christoffer also stayed still, unblinking. Zaria too stood motionless, for dramatic effect. Hector gently pushed the boys to prove they were unmoving.

King Flein licked a finger, reached out and touched the inside of Aleks' ear, giving him a Wet Willie. The king laughed enjoying his prank. "How wonderful! How long does it last?"

"Until you turn it off, your Majesty," Zaria said, stepping forward, breaking the illusion she'd been frozen too.

Prince Floki who'd looked smug a minute before, now sat there with his mouth agape in disbelief. "You were frozen too. I saw it. This is a trick."

"No trick," Zaria said, stepping forward toward the thrones. "Now, may I please have the Drakeland Sword? It is rightfully mine, after all."

"No," Floki said. "This is a trick. You're clearly an elf, or fey, or even ellefolken. Come here."

"She is none of those things," Hector said, exasperated. "I vouch for her."

"I don't believe it. Come here, girl," Floki commanded, snapping his fingers.

Zaria looked over her shoulder at Hector. He glowered unhelpfully at the prince, giving Zaria no indication of what to do. She stepped toward the prince. He grabbed her arm and yanked her close.

She struggled and pushed at his shoulders. "Let me go, you oaf!"

"Don't touch her," Hector shouted, striding forward menacingly. He was blocked by the guards.

The prince ran his jeweled fingers over her scalp, snagging her hair and pinching her ears. It hurt. Zaria beat on his shoulders, and kicked his shin. With a pain-filled yelp, Floki let her go.

She backed away hurriedly and jumped off the dais. Dodging the guards, Zaria rushed back to Hector. He wrapped an arm around her shoulder and glared at the dwarf rulers.

"That was uncalled for," he said. "Are you satisfied that her ears are round and her head isn't sporting antlers?"

"Yes," Floki said mulishly, rubbing his aching shin.

King Flein laughed, punched his son in the arm, and tossed the stargazer to Hector, who caught it deftly.

"Your point is proven, Stag Lord," Flein said. "You can turn the device off, and I'll arrange for the sword to be delivered to her room later this evening. In the meantime enjoy our hospitality."

"Thank you," Hector said. "We won't be staying long. We'll leave on the morrow."

"That still leaves tonight," the king said. "Have fun, explore. Don't get lost though. We've many tunnels and many dead ends."

Nodding, Hector released the boys from the stargazer's hold and handed it back to Aleks. As Aleks took it, he grimaced and swiped at his ear. The disgusted look on his face was priceless.

"Did it work?" Christoffer asked Zaria conspiratorially, as they left the receiving chamber.

She smiled, relieved and pleased. "Yes, although Floki thought it was a trick."

"Figures he would," Christoffer said, slinging an arm over her shoulders. "Now what?"

"Now we shop for supplies," Hector said. "I vaguely remember where the market was."

Geirr pointed to Aleks. "He will know."

Aleks nodded when Hector looked his way. "I know how to find it."

"Lead on," Hector invited.

With Aleks' uncanny ability to navigate, the group got to the marketplace quickly, not once having to back track or detour. Filip and Geirr wanted to explore the weapons shop and raced ahead. Zaria wanted to look into the book store, but hesitated to go in, until Hector waved them off.

"I'm going to get food stuffs," he said, indicating the shop with colorful awnings to their right. "I hope you all like reindeer jerky."

"That just sounds wrong," Christoffer said. "Aren't you an elk? Doesn't that make it the same thing as cannibalism?"

"No," Hector said, amused. "Meet me back here in about an hour."

As Zaria was about to enter Small and Tall Tales, Aleks yanked her away and down another corridor. Christoffer followed, not caring where they shopped.

"I wanted to look at the books," Zaria protested. "Where are you taking us?"

"To the magic shop," he said. "We might find things we need there."

The trio stopped in front of the Hidden Gem. Its sign was as opulent as any other on the street, but the store felt shabby. Its windows were small and smudged, the door was scuffed at the bottom, and a spider spun its web lazily over the door. They ducked under the web.

Christoffer pushed the door open, and it creaked ominously. Zaria crept in behind him and ducked into the nearby shelves. Aleks joined her and peered at a collection of teacups. Christoffer went across the row to the other side and examined a set of keys there. Everything was covered in dust.

"Why hello, dearies," a disembodied voice said, startling them.

"Who are you?" Christoffer demanded, standing on tip-toe and peering over the shelving.

"The proprietor, you darling boy," an old dwarf woman said, shuffling into view. She was covered in a kaleidoscope of layered shawls. Their fanciful designs were muted and graying from age. "You may call me Granny."

"What makes these items magical?" Zaria asked, holding up a pair of scissors. "They look like ordinary objects."

"Of course they are, sweetheart." Granny gestured for Zaria to hand her the scissors. "These are very fine tailor shears. Why I remember the young fellow who came in and sold them to me. He said the cloths they could cut were so fine, they were practically see-through. The final clothes were the envy of royalty. I don't have the complete set anymore sadly. If you were to acquire the thimble and needle, why, your clothes would practically make themselves!"

"And these?" Christoffer said, showing the box of keys.

"Those are keys that can't be lost. However they've been a bit glitchy lately. Some of their owners lose them, but instead of returning home the keys return to the box."

"And the tea set?" asked Aleks.

"Brews a flawless cup of tea every time. You don't even have to pour water into it. You can fill it up with whatever you like. Although, I should warn you, the last owner put in poison to test that out and died. The tea however was brewed perfectly."

"Do you mind, if we browse?" Zaria asked.

"Oh course not, sweetheart, you and your friends go right on ahead. If you need me, I'll be on my stool."

They watched as Granny shuffled back to her seat by a little hearth and sat down. She pulled a pile of knitting onto her lap and started to hum off key as her needles flashed quickly.

Zaria wandered further into the store and picked up bits and bobs to examine. The various curios that intrigued her were a mangled quill, a paper weight, and a spyglass. Aleks had in his hands a pile of string, a lantern, and a compass.

"What?" he demanded at Zaria's quizzical look. "Can't I want a compass?"

"Why would you need one?" she asked.

Christoffer found them and laughed. He plucked the compass from Aleks and added it to his collection, which included a mirror, a necklace, and a single boot.

They brought their treasures to the old dwarf woman. She set aside her needles and hummed in delight over their selections. She picked each item up and brought it closer to her face, squinting.

"Very fine things indeed," said Granny. She picked up the mangled quill Zaria had found. "This quill, for instance, brings the written word to life. Too bad the author was trampled by a mammoth. I don't know what he was thinking, writing about a stampede."

"Oh well, maybe not that one then," Zaria said, pulling it from the stack.

"Are you sure, darling girl? It's one of a kind. No? Well, okay. Take this mirror, it allows you to see loved ones at any distance and maybe even talk to them, but I haven't tried it."

"Is there a catch?" Christoffer asked.

"I don't believe so. Would you like to try it out? Who would you like to see?"

"Uh," Christoffer said, scratching his neck. "Maybe later. What about the boot?"

"One half of the seven-league boots," Granny said proudly. "You'd have to hobble or hop but it would be manageable. It won't resize to your foot though, unless you have the other one. You'd have to be careful when you took a step, or you might lose it and be stuck somewhere."

"Don't you have anything that's complete?" Aleks asked grumpily. "This string perhaps?"

"Well, it's self-threading. Do you need help threading, dearie? Your clothes look all right to me."

"Never mind," Aleks said, putting the objects on the table. "We must really be going."

"Could you get my spectacles first before you go?" Granny asked.

"I'd be happy to," said Zaria. "Where are they?"

"Over there I think," Granny said waving in the opposite corner. Zaria walked over, found them and brought them back. "Thank you, sweetheart."

Granny slipped them on and looked up. Zaria just managed not to jump out of her skin in fright. Her heart pounded. Staring back at her superimposed on the lenses was not Granny's watery eyes, but the horrible thing's glowing eyes. Zaria didn't think twice, she grabbed the boys and raced for the door, pushing through it like a horde of trolls was chasing them.

***

The sword was delivered to Zaria's chamber after supper. It was wrapped in heavy velvet and tied with silk tassels. She thanked the guards and shut the door, carrying the sword to the bed, where she unwrapped and examined it from pommel to point. She ran her thumb along the edge, and it sang out.

The Drakeland Sword possessed a deadly beauty. Its hilt was decorated with silver imagery of dwarves fighting dragons, embedded with amethyst gems and pearls. The blade had Nordic writing engraved all over it. The sword felt light and wielded easily in her hands.

Zaria pretended to be an heroic knight and gave a few practice slashes at the air. "Stay back, you cur, or I'll run you through."

It wasn't quite balanced in one hand. Securing it between two hands, she again jabbed the sword at her imaginary opponent. "Take that, and that, and that."

The door opened startling her, and Zaria dropped the sword. It landed in the dirt with a dull clatter. Embarrassed, she stooped to pick it up. Turning around she saw Hector. He smiled tiredly.

"No need to be embarrassed, Princess. It is your mother's sword. Are you packed for the morning? We'll leave at first light."

"Is Hart far away? Will we be able to free him tomorrow?"

Hector touched the cord of the necklace around his neck. "It's warmer – the heart – which is good. We are near where I last found him. If all goes well, he will be free soon."

"How does the necklace work?" Zaria asked, wrapping the sword up and placing it beside her bed. She sat down on the duvet.

Hector wandered back toward the door. "When you hold it to the light, it casts a beam. Follow the beam, and you'll find Hart."

"But how is it bound to him?" she pressed, biting her lower lip.

"Old magic, from long ago. It is passed from father to son. After a few days the necklace realigns itself with the new wearer."

Zaria tilted her head, confused. "But you've been wearing it for months!"

"The magic doesn't work backwards. It can't be transferred from son to father."

"Oh."

"Good night, Princess. Thank you for helping me retrieve the Drakeland Sword."

"Good night, Hector. It was the right thing to do."

After Hector left, Zaria got ready for bed. Just before she turned off the lights, she gave the sword a pat. Her heart was full of hope, and she just knew they were going to rescue Hart. Nothing, not even an ugly river-troll would be able to stop them.

Zaria's dreams were interrupted in the most unpleasant way. She recognized that foul breath instantly. Without hesitation she grabbed the sword and sat straight up in bed, waiting for her eyes to adjust.

When they did, she saw it. Backlit from the torches in the corridor stood the trollish specter, the terror that stalked her – the thing with half her face – dressed in a copy of her blue pajamas. It smiled wickedly from the doorway. It was leaving. That did not ease her fear; it heightened it. What had he done?

"Olaf will be pleased," it taunted. "Yer terror is just what we needed to free Koll, and now I have it."

"I'm not afraid of you," Zaria said, quaking in the bedclothes. She gripped the sword tighter. "I'm not afraid of you."

"Yer too late. Ye lose, Princess," it cackled and slammed the door, shutting Zaria in the dark.

Chapter Fourteen:
Liberating Hart

Zaria threw off the sheets and leapt from the bed. She hurriedly pulled her jacket over her fox pajamas and stuffed her feet into her sneakers, not bothering to lace them. Clutching the sword to her chest, she raced to the door and throwing it open, stared down the stone hallway, looking in both directions. There, at the end of the hall with a glint of gold, the specter slipped away.

She raced to follow it. She knew from Hector that Olaf needed four things to free Koll – Hart, to trap

Hector in his current form, so the Stag Lord couldn't reverse the rot of the Golden Kings; a way to remove her mother's shoes, to cross the bridge into the Under Realm; the Drakeland Sword to break the chains binding Koll to the realm; and her.

If her fear would release Koll, or give him power over others, she had to stop the specter from delivering it to the dragon. The sword was designed to fell dragons; it could fell this awful creature too. She wouldn't let it escape. Too much was at stake.

The trollish specter noticed her following and cackled, putting on speed. Zaria huffed and puffed and pushed herself to run faster. She followed it out to the main marketplace of Jerndor. The streets were gloomy, the light dampened. She pulled a torch from the wall and dashed across the courtyard where the fountain was off.

"Ye can't catch me, Princess," it jeered, ducking into a set of tunnels she hadn't been down.

Zaria refused to give up. She followed blindly, barely keeping up with its fast pace. Left, right, right, right, left, right, left. Beyond lost, she traveled deeper into Jerndor. Torches were no longer lit along the walls. She was grateful she'd thought to snag one from the main courtyard. It cast enough light to lift the oppressing gloom.

The specter moved like a flickering shadow in the dark. She followed the echo of its dull footfalls slapping against the earthen floor. When the echo stopped, Zaria slowed, limping along and breathing harshly. She couldn't hear anything over the sound of her breathing. She held her breath, lifted the torch, and peered gingerly around a corner.

It was a dead end, with a cracked mirror guarding its far wall. Zaria took a moment to unsheathe the sword, dropping the heavy velvet, which pooled into a pile of fabric at her feet. Holding the sword in one hand, point-down, and the torch in her other hand, Zaria pressed forward.

At the mirror, she examined her reflection. Lifting the torch higher, Zaria ran her gaze over everything the light touched. The mirror was aged, covered in black-brown spots, like it was rusting. The frame was golden, thick, heavy, and ornate. She ran a hand over its surface and found her fingers sliding inside. The cool wet-dry treacly feeling caused goosebumps to erupt on her skin.

Zaria looked behind her, hesitating. Should she find help? No. It was too late for help. Besides, who would believe her? Ghosts didn't exist. Nobody had ever seen it but her. It was time to face it down and take away its power – the ability to make her fear it.

She pushed through the mirror and emerged on the other side. She blinked, and then blinked again. She had materialized in an oddly familiar space. The scene before her was like a memory of Gloomwood Forest, at once both similar and distinct.

Twisted tree trunks crowded close together. Many were dark and black, charred from a long ago fire. In the distance she could make out a burbling river. She glanced at the mirror behind her and saw the back of her head. She jumped.

So did her reflection, though it never turned around. That made her uneasy. Zaria reached out to touch the smooth glass and saw her reflection do the same. Her fingers met the mirror, but didn't sink through it. She pulled back.

Zaria turned back toward the forest, analyzing her options. She used her shoe to gouge a small hole in the ground and placed the torch in it, packing the dirt around it to keep it in place. She would need the torch when she came back and figured out how to return to Jerndor.

Using two hands on the sword, Zaria crept forward. She glided dream-like through the scene. A hazy white mist blew toward her, creeping over the ground. She wished it was Norwick, Hector's pet winter-wyvern. She could use a friendly presence in this unfriendly place.

A little deeper into the woods, Zaria found the river. It was slow-moving and sluggish. Silver light flashed inside its shallow depths. Zaria knew before she looked that the dancing flashes of light would be glinting off of knives swimming in the river. She was right.

That meant she had to be near Gloomwood Forest! This same river flowed through a beautiful golden glade, home to generations of ellefolken kings. Those silent Golden Kings had guarded a precious treasure – Hector's son Hart. The mirror had transported Zaria a great distance south.

Would Olaf be so foolish as to hide Hart in his people's forest? Zaria didn't understand any of it. She looked left and right, following the line of the river with her eyes. A short distance away she spotted shoe prints in the mud. She headed for them.

Crouching down to look at them, Zaria had to laugh at herself. What did she know about tracking anything? The prints in the mud weren't hidden and were very deep. Despite the mist, they would be easy to follow. So that's what she did.

It wasn't until a keen bugling noise broke the silence, that Zaria realized how silent the forest had been. Beside her, the river was the only thing moving and making noise, until it faded like white noise in her consciousness.

Nothing else moved. Wind did not blow through the tree trunks. Animals did not chatter. Even shadows didn't move. It was like the space was stuck permanently in twilight.

"Where am I?" she wondered aloud. "This is all so strange."

The bugling cry came again, triggering a memory.

"Hart?" Zaria called out.

The same sad cry blew again. Zaria picked up her pace. When she realized the tracks she'd been following led straight to the wounded cry, Zaria's heart thumped hollowly in her chest. What would she find when she reached the end of the tracks?

She didn't have to wait long to discover the answer. The banks of the river widened, pressing the trees further back. A miserable animal was staked to the ground and swaddled in chains. Zaria recognized it immediately.

"HART!" she shouted, running the last dozen feet to her friend.

She dropped to her knees, and wrapped an arm around his neck, careful not to let go of the sword. She still didn't know what had happened to the specter she'd been chasing. It was around here somewhere. She could feel it watching them. She would not give it the opportunity to steal the sword.

Zaria gripped Hart tighter, breathing in his warm earthy scent. He bugled softly, jerking his neck from her grasp. She ran a hand over his hide.

"Easy, Hart, it's just me. Zaria."

She studied her friend. His eyes were nearly the same golden color as his antlers. They were not as sad as she remembered. Determination and fight shone in them and a gleam of something else. She was relieved. He had not given up.

The rest of him, though, was in bad shape. Wherever the chains held him, his pure white fur was tinged red with blood. The sight hurt Zaria. Her chest ached. He'd clearly struggled for a long time.

Months and months. Eight months to be exact. It was all her fault. She did this. It didn't matter that she'd been tricked into trading the elk for her friend. Or that Olaf was to blame. In her heart, Zaria knew Hart could never forgive her.

"I'm going to get you out of this," she told him. "I have the Drakeland Sword." She hefted it up to show him. "Keep an eye out for trouble. I followed something here."

Hart nodded and struggled to stand up. Zaria stood too and walked over to the stake in the ground. She adjusted her grip on the sword and gave a practice swing.

"Ready?" she asked Hart.

He pawed the ground with golden hooves, snorting enthusiastically and tossing his antlers around.

"I'll take that as a yes," she laughed. "Here goes nothing."

She swung the sword. The chain broke apart in a shower of rainbow-colored sparkles. When the shimmering stopped, she saw that the piece of chain connected to the stake had turned into an array of tiny gemstones. The chain that wrapped around Hart, though, was still silver and pulsing with magic.

Zaria crossed back to Hart and began untangling the chain. It was awkward with one hand, but she refused to put the sword down. If she let it go and the specter stole it, then Olaf would only need two things to free Koll: a pair of Helena's shoes so he could enter the Under Realm and a way to take the shoes off afterward so he and the dragon could get back into the real world.

As more of the chain was removed, her friend began breathing easier. Zaria threw the last of it in a heap on the ground, stood back and smiled broadly at Hart.

"You're free!" she said happily. "Can you walk? Let's get going."

She turned around and began walking. Her heart was ten pounds lighter. She'd done it. She'd done it. She'd freed Hart.

"Hector is going to be so pleased. I just know —"

"Stupid Princess," a voice said behind her. "Yer not going anywhere."

Zaria turned and stared blankly at the specter. She looked back for Hart. He was nowhere to be seen. She faced off against her troll doppelganger. She refused to be cowed by the specter's presence ever again.

"Where's Hart?" she demanded. "What did you do with him? Hart! Hart!"

"Hart's with Olaf. As he's always been."

"No," Zaria said angrily. "He was right here. I just removed the chains binding him to that stake."

"Ye don't get it, do ye?" it said. "Ye will. I really should thank ye Princess for freeing me. I've spent too long trapped down here in yer mother's realm."

Zaria shook her head. "I don't understand. You've been following me everywhere this whole time. What are you talking about?"

It tilted its head. Then slowly, like watching a candle melt, the thing before her shifted. In the place of the ugly troll version of her face, stood a handsome man with wavy black hair, a full beard, and a thick mustache. He looked like a darker version of Hector.

"I'm Koll," he said.

"No," Zaria denied. "No. No. No. You can't be. It doesn't make sense."

Koll spread his hands out. "Olaf weakened the Golden Kings, allowing me to slip the smallest piece of myself out of the Under Realm. Persistence brought us here."

"You were Hart just now," Zaria accused, looking at the ground behind where Koll stood.

Her gaze fixed on his wing-tipped shoes. They were golden, just like the trollish specter's sneakers had been, just like Hart's hooves... She struggled to remember if Hart had golden hooves eight months ago. With a sinking feeling, she realized that he hadn't. They'd been black. The golden shoes were Helena's charmed shoes, meant to keep the dragons in the Under Realm. The last vestiges of hope withered away when she noticed the tracks of the specter and Hart disappearing. As she watched they vanished one by one until only hers were left.

"He wasn't here at all," she said softly, horrified.

"Not even for a moment," Koll said mildly, pleasantly, almost sympathetically. He stooped to pick up the chain, fingering it calculatingly. "Now, it's time to keep ye from tattle-telling to the others. Then, I plan to take yer place."

"Y-y-you can't do that. You're not convincing enough," Zaria stammered, backing away.

"Not yet," he said. "But it won't take much. Ye've fed me much of yer power without realizing it."

"What," she said aghast. "What do you mean?"

"Haven't ye wondered why ye can't produce a lick of magic?" Koll asked, laughing at her, mocking her ignorance. "Hector should have realized, but he's had much on his mind. Take a look around ye, all the Golden Kings here have fallen. He's so focused on retrieving Hart so he can do his duty to bolster these defenses that he's missed the forest for the trees."

"How can you steal my magic?" Zaria asked.

"Through yer fear," he explained, walking toward her slowly. "It's like pulling saltwater taffy, at first everything is stiff and unyielding, but with a little encouragement the whole process becomes smooth and pliant. Each time we met, I could escape mentally a little more from my prison. But none of this would have been possible, if ye didn't let me in."

"I let you in?" Zaria whispered, fear gripping her heart. "How?"

"Yer anger and self-pity over Hart," Koll said, tilting his head to examine her. "It was like a door was left open in yer mind. First, I slipped into yer dreams, then into yer waking hours. It was all a mental exercise and the more real I became to ye, the more convincingly I could interact with ye. Even the tracks leading ye here are fake. I couldn't move from my circle until ye broke the chains binding me."

"So that's why nobody else saw you," Zaria said, dismayed. "You were never there. You just made me think you were."

Koll smiled brightly. "Now ye get it."

"What did you promise Olaf to get him to help you?"

Koll raised a sardonic brow. "That's what ye want to know?" he asked in derision. "Very well. I promised him the Gjöll. It was his originally, which he remembers. What he doesn't remember is that he lost it due to his selfless desire to secure the Under Realm. Without a river-troll to wield it, the Gjöll reverts to wild protection magic, nobody can cross it, not even by the damn bridge, unless aided by light magic."

Shocked to learn that Olaf wasn't always the bad guy, Zaria scrambled to understand. "Why doesn't he remember? Did you make him forget?"

"Hmm-mm," Koll confirmed. "I might not give it back though. Olaf still has to find a way to rid me of these cursed shoes so I can cross the Gjallarbrú and return home, where I belong."

He examined the chain in his hands and judged the distance between them. Zaria tensed, alarmed by the gleam in his eyes. Koll relaxed his stance. She watched him warily.

"You don't belong in the world," Zaria said, shrieking a little as she dodged his steady pursuit. "I'm going to warn everyone." She ducked behind a tree.

"We'll see about that," Koll sneered, his charm melting away like crayons in the sun.

His features shifted again returning his appearance once more to the creature of her nightmares. He lunged for her. Zaria shrieked and jumped out of the way. She landed on her ankle, and it buckled under her. She collapsed in a heap.

Scrambling to get her bearings, Zaria chanced a glance behind her. Koll tossed the chain at her. Reflexively, she batted it away. It fell harmless to her right. She tried to stand, but her foot would not support her weight. Zaria bit back a cry of despair.

"It's all over now, Princess. Quit struggling. It won't do ye any good," Koll said, retrieving the chain from the ground.

He was right. It didn't matter how powerful Koll was, he could be as weak as a mouse, and she still wouldn't be able to beat him. She didn't have magic. He'd stolen that. She couldn't even stand up. She was worse than useless.

Worse still, she'd helped him win his freedom. She'd cut him loose herself! How stupid could she be? Now he was going to assume her place and convince all of her friends that he was her. He would get away with it, too, for who could stop him?

A bright light flashed in the twilight, blinding Zaria, but also blinding Koll. Zaria crawled on the ground, and slipped behind some of the trees which she realized were actually the roots. She pressed her back against the burnt husk of a long ago Golden King and tried to steady her breathing and her heart.

She blinked back tears and looked at the world around her with new eyes. The Golden Kings' roots had grown so deep, and stood sentinel for so long that they appeared like trees in the Under Realm. Even as strong as they were, they couldn't resist Koll's evil influence forever.

"Don't give up," a fierce feminine voice shouted from above.

Zaria looked up and saw a radiant woman in the tree's tangled roots. Her mouth dropped open. The woman looked like an older version of her, with rich tawny skin that seemed to glow; dark sable hair, sleek and thick, pulled back into an elaborate up-do; and bright vivid purple eyes burning with magic and power.

"Get up, Zaria," the woman said, encouraging her. "You're stronger than you think."

"Queen Helena, yer here," Koll said, his voice betraying a hint of worry. "No matter, it's too late. I'm free thanks to yer daughter. She's such a pleasantly terrified little thing."

"Run to the mirror," Helena commanded, dropping from the trees to the forest floor.

Zaria looked between her mother and the dragon. Where light emanated like a beacon around Queen Helena, darkness seeped from Koll, creating a twilight haze thick with magic.

"Zaria, go," Helena's voice grew stern. "I can handle him. Warn the others."

Zaria scrambled to her feet, sword still in hand. She looked at it and at her mother, then back at Koll. He watched them steadily, wearing a nasty smirk. She held the Drakeland Sword out to Helena. It was her mother's after all, and she could use it against Koll better than Zaria could.

Helena pushed it away. "Take it. You're going to need it."

"What about you?" Zaria cried. "Koll has the chains. How are you going to defeat him?"

"Yeah, Sorceress," Koll taunted, mimicking Zaria's voice. He was getting better at it. "How will ye win against me now? Ye don't have yer little army of friends to back ye up this time."

Helena shot a fistful of white magic at his face. Koll bellowed and clawed at his eyes. "With magic," she answered. "Zaria, do as I say and run! Now!"

Helena threw a ball of magic at Zaria, pushing her away. Zaria tripped, but righted herself before she could fall again. She limped to the next tree and clung to it. Loud booms echoed behind her. She peered back and saw that Koll had shifted into his dragon form.

He was massive, almost as tall as the Under Realm. Black and red scales covered him from snout to tail. His talons were wickedly long and curved like scimitars. Jagged spikes ran along his spine like broken teeth. Evil yellow eyes skewered all they saw with contempt.

He shot a ball of fire at her mother. Water met it and vaporized in an instant, causing another boom. As Zaria watched, Helena glanced over and tossed another ball of magic at her. Zaria scrambled out of the way, feeling a warm blast of air along her cheek.

Stumbling along, Zaria traced the river back to the magic mirror. Koll told the truth, his tracks were fake. She saw none on the way back.

Tears leaked from her eyes as she ran, obscuring her vision. Her nose clogged in minutes, forcing her to breathe through her mouth. Each inhalation squeezed past a wall of fire in her lungs.

The battle raged behind her. Magic crisscrossed the sky, like a violent ballet of color. Purples. Reds. Whites. Blacks. Distant thunder echoed every time the magic collided. Zaria forced herself to keep going. She was almost there.

When she reached the mirror, Zaria was a sopping mess. She plucked the torch from its spot in the ground and stared at the mirror. She still saw only the back of her head, but in the mirror, behind her reflection, or in front of it – she didn't know which was accurate – she could see light flickering in the stone hall.

"Hey," Zaria sobbed, hiccupping. "Hey! Over here!"

She pounded on the mirror, but the light dimmed as the person moved away. Zaria kicked the mirror, and instantly regretted it.

"Ow," she whimpered, hugging her toe.

She hobbled around the mirror and cried in relief. On the other side, she was mirrored normally. Never was she so happy to see her face. Zaria reached out and touched her reflection. Her fingers slipped coolly through the surface and she followed suit, emerging into the relative safety of Jerndor.

Epilogue: The Dragon Ahead

"Help," Zaria shouted. "Somebody help! Please, please help!"

Hector and Christoffer raced around the corner with two armored dwarves.

"Zaria," Christoffer cried out, racing toward her.

"We found her," Hector shouted down the hallway. "She's safe."

Zaria threw her arms around Christoffer and cried big fat ugly tears. Christoffer took the torch from her and handed it to a dwarf. She tried explaining what happened, but she couldn't get out a single coherent sentence. Hector peeled her away from her friend and gave her a little shake.

"What happened, Princess?" he asked.

Zaria gestured to the mirror, and managed to choke out a single understandable word. "Koll."

Hector looked at the trolls. "That mirror doesn't lead into the Under Realm does it?"

The dwarves looked to each other and shrugged. "I don't know, Stag Lord. Nobody's been down this far in ages."

"Break it," Hector commanded. "Do it now."

"No, you can't," Zaria gasped. "My mom's down there."

"Queen Helena?" Hector asked. She nodded. "Then it is a mirror to the dragons. We can't afford to leave it standing."

The dwarves didn't hesitate. The one not holding the torch, grabbed his sword, and the two charged the mirror. In a simultaneous blow the mirror shattered, flying into a thousand pieces. The shards rained to the ground in a shimmering, tinkling, wall of crystalline.

"We must tell King Flein what has happened," one of the guards said, sweating nervously.

"Yes," Hector said. "We'll be right there. I'm very interested in knowing how such a dangerous object existed."

"Could Koll have escaped the Under Realm by the mirror?" Christoffer asked, confused and trying to catch up.

"Physically? No, not if he is chained. Mentally is a different story."

"H-he isn't," Zaria hiccupped. She rubbed her jacket's sleeve against her nose. "He isn't chained. I freed him."

"You did what?" Hector asked, shocked.

"I didn't mean to! I was chasing the specter that's been haunting me. The one nobody sees."

"There's no such thing as ghosts," Hector said, shaking his head. "Nothing could, as you say, haunt you."

"Well, it could, and it did. The it being Koll, as I found out," Zaria retorted. "Or a piece of him."

"A piece of him? How?" Hector looked at her blankly and then at the broken mirror shards around them. "Oh… oh no." Hector sank against the wall. "He's been able to restore some of his lost power."

"From me," Zaria confirmed. "That's why I can't do magic."

"So you chased Koll into the mirror…" Hector prompted, pinching the bridge of his nose.

"A piece of him, and he was disguised. He was pretending to be a troll version of me. I didn't know it was him. I found myself in what looked like Gloomwood Forest. I found Hart… except it wasn't Hart. It was Koll again. I freed Hart, but I didn't. It was Koll."

Christoffer wrapped an arm around her shoulders. "It's not your fault. Dragons are master manipulators. Everyone has said so."

Zaria stomped her foot. "It is. It is my fault."

"No, Princess," Hector denied swiftly. "It's mine. You said you saw your mother?"

Zaria nodded. "Helena told me to run back to the mirror. I tried to give her the sword, but she said I needed to keep it."

"At least she's alive, that gives me hope. Don't worry, Princess. Your mother is strong. She'll survive until we can go to her aid. Come," Hector beckoned, striding away. "We need to talk to Flein immediately."

Christoffer and Zaria hurried to catch up. As they rounded the corner, they ran into the others. Filip took the sword and handed it to Aleks, then gave her a hug. That brought on a fresh wave of tears.

"What happened?" Geirr asked, looking to Hector.

"Zaria was tricked. Koll is free," Christoffer summarized.

"Holy cow," Geirr said, staring wide-eyed in shock as Zaria sniffed valiantly, trying to regain her composure.

"The dragon ahead would be challenging enough," Hector began, "but he isn't stupid. He knows Zaria will warn us and that we will come with numbers. Koll will free his brothers and try to break out through the Golden Kings, if he can't rid himself of the shoes. The circle is nearly rotten to the core, it won't hold for much longer. We must rescue Hart. There is no time to lose."

Thanks for Reading

Thank you for reading the Zaria Fierce trilogy. If you enjoyed Zaria Fierce and the Enchanted Drakeland Sword, please share it with your friends, family, coworkers, and strangers! Consider writing a review on Amazon or Goodreads to help other readers discover Zaria and her friends on their journeys through magical Norway.

The Adventure Continues

Zaria Fierce and the
Dragon Keeper's Golden Shoes

Get a sneak peek of the next book in the Zaria Fierce Trilogy at: http://keiragillett.com/golden-shoes/

About the Author: Keira Gillett

Keira Gillett is a technical publications librarian, book blogger, world traveler, artist, and now author. She graduated from the University of Florida with a Bachelor of Arts in Drawing and Painting. From an early age her mother instilled a love of the written word, as such she has always been an avid reader. She's excited to share her love of reading and Zaria Fierce with the world.

Find her at http://keiragillett.com/

About the Artist:
Eoghan Kerrigan

Eoghan Kerrigan is an illustrator from Kildare, Ireland who draws primarily fantasy characters and creatures. He studied illustration in Ballyfermot College of Further Education and has produced work for various independent projects. He has two cats and a soft spot for trolls.

Find him at http://eoghankerrigan.blogspot.ie/

www.ingramcontent.com/pod-product-compliance
Lightning Source LLC
Chambersburg PA
CBHW030400020726
47493CB00003B/889